MW00470977

MOTORMAN

MOTORMAN
by David Ohle

3rd bed
Providence, RI
2004

Motorman
Published by 3rd bed

Copyright ©1971, 1972, 2004 by David Ohle.
First 3rd bed paperback edition, 2004.
First Alfred A. Knopf, Inc., cloth edition, 1972.
Portions of this novella have appeared in different
form in the *Transatlantic Review* and *Esquire*.
All rights reserved.

ISBN 0-9709428-2-6
PCN 2004103347
3rd bed, Inc., is a not-for-profit 501(c)3
Corporation. All contributions are
tax-deductible to the extent allowed by law.
www.3rdbed.com

Design, layout, and typesetting
by Ambivalent Design.
Cover art by Matt Tracy.
Printed by United Graphics.

The publisher wishes to thank
Matthew Derby, Brian Evenson,
Joanna Howard, and Ben Marcus
for their help with the project.

Introduction

For a long time I was scared to read *Motorman*. It had come recommended to me in such hushed tones that it sounded disruptively incendiary and illegal. Not only would the reader of this crazed novel burn to ashes, apparently, but he might be posthumously imprisoned for reading the book—a jar of cinder resting in a jail cell. Books were not often spoken of so potently to me, as contraband, as narcotic, as ordnance. There was the whispered promise that my mind would be blown after reading *Motorman*. There was the assurance that once I read it I would drool with awe, writerly awe, the awe of watching a madman master at work, David Ohle, awesomely carving deep, black holes into the edifice of the English language.

I was, to say the least, guarded and jealous of it in advance, protesting the very idea of *Motorman*. Its existence bothered me, and I grew leery of being artistically paralyzed by its reported high oddity and invention, its completely unexampled decimation of fiction-as-we-have-come-to-know-it. At the time, when I and the few writers I knew fantasized more about *how* readers might react to what we wrote than *what* exactly we might write—our readers would be sprung aloft and unable to land, rendered gummy and mute, form an army, start a new language, or simply melt into malleable form so that we could use this "reader spackle" to build an outdoor shelter in Duluth—Ohle's reader response behavior was the pinnacle of what I thought could be achieved. His fans were so serene. In non-confrontational tones, they could casually remark that he was the best out there, the strangest, oddest, most original fiction writer no one had ever heard of. The most dismaying aspect of their allegiance was their seeming indifference to whether or not I ever read the novel—in fact, it seemed that they might prefer it if I refrained. More spoils for them, after all. Too many readers might ruin the book. This anti-missionary approach turns out to be the best recruiting tactic of all. Ohle's readers behaved as if they never had to read another inventive fiction writer again. They had read the sort of book that finally satisfied the thirst, a final book that could behave as a sort of source bible for anything that might come afterward—the creation text for all new fiction. I might try to tell them about some other writer, possibly equally as obscure, intense, and wild, and they would listen politely, say "huh," and then assure me that whoever I was lamely sponsoring had nothing on Ohle. Ohle was onto some sublime weirdness that he achieved so easily it was as if he was writing behind his own back. His very sentences seemed equipped with tracers that generated secondary and tertiary amazements in the wake of the primary spectacle. Ohle was the dogsbody that resulted from a glandular mishap between Flann O'Brien, Leonora Carrington, Philip K. Dick, Raymond Chandler, Borges, and Raymond Roussel. That is, if those writers had all been alive at the same time and partying together at the same organ swap.

And the kicker was always the rumor (still unverified) that Ohle worked in Kansas for William S. Burroughs, transcribing the man's dreams every morning.

In other words, David Ohle was reported to be the custodian for the subconscious of William S. Burroughs.

One might fittingly wonder what that job interview was like, but that is a curiosity best saved for another time. One suspects, soon perhaps, a rash of one-act plays to bring the idea to life for us.

I finally read *Motorman*, cautiously, moving through its dark pages with a mixture of suspicion and anxiety, waiting for aphasia to strike. I soon discovered the book to be more suspicious and anxious than I was, swollen with a mixture of dread and apathy, a world that showed a healthy disrespect for physics and the laws of biology. But not sci-fi. Not magical realist. Not anything but itself. It was far more story-driven than I expected it to be, much more located in a character and his struggles, even if that character had four sheep's hearts inside his chest and had a penchant for smoking stonepicks. I must have been expecting, in the pages of *Motorman*, a new alphabet, a demanding, unintelligible, ferociously experimental and annihilating text that would bitch-slap my language processing abilities until I had succumbed to a boneless heap on my reader's carpet, moaning in Spanish. But I discovered an oddly tender book that used imagination as an afterthought, however potently, as if beautiful fires on the horizon are precisely the backdrop that might restore life to our identity-quest stories and make us care again about the most elemental things. Extreme imagination, for Ohle, was simply the atmosphere in which a primal story of loss could breathe most freely.

I did not die or even catch fire during this bout of reading, although I did discover that Ohle had created, if not an influence over the fiction that would come after *Motorman*, then a shadow that could not be ignored, a reminder that some of our most provocative directions in fiction are too intense and scorching to be followed by others. So while it might be true that Ohle burned the road after him, that heat has cooled enough for a new generation to travel over it, to once again read a groundbreaking book that looks no less novel now, over thirty years after it first appeared. Thanks to this heroic reprint by 3rd bed, his older admirers can once again sponsor him to a new legion of readers, and the Ohle vocabulary and scaffolding can re-enter the bloodstream of the culture.

It is curious that a reprint could be heroic. It is more curious that a book this good could go out of print so quickly. And it is most curious that an introduction would even be required for a novel that, if you examine it carefully in the right kind of light, might actually be seen to be *steaming*.

I would venture that had *Motorman* not been *published*, but instead *shown* at an art gallery, page by page plastered to the walls maybe, its cachet and value would not be in question, and Ohle would now be regarded as a vital conceptual artist of the seventies, akin to someone who built a behavior cannon out of bent plywood that pelted pedestrians with one of the seven leading emotions, each emotion equipped with a fur backing and a set of workable teeth. That Ohle did something like this, but purely with language, eschewing bricks and mortar, seems even more amazing, yet it's not something that usually happens in a book, and this might partially account for its resulting obscurity. When a book gets called "experimental," you can hear a ghetto opening up to swallow it, the sound of a few nickels falling into the author's pocket, whereas experimentation is a given in visual and other kinds of art. It is expected. Without it there is regionalism, or, more simply, crap. Without fevered ambition, you have competent seascapes hanging in the hotel lobby, ass-relaxing music playing in the elevator. Without the desire to produce something unexampled in the art form, you have books that are cynical blueprints for the movies that will bring them to life. You have characters with beards playing hockey.

Visual artists have critics, ostensibly, while innovative writers have, for the most part, reviewers, whose job it is ever more frequently to determine the cost-benefit of purchasing the book, using heart-crushing standards such as beachtime readability, difficulty, sameness, narrative drive, and superficiality (more, please!). Or they are hen-pecked jacket copy plagiarists, dutifully paraphrasing publicist's pitch letters in their newspapers. But rather than remark on the obvious cultural conditions (or lack thereof) that have rendered many artistic writers (as opposed to, uh, other kinds of writers) marginal, based on their low sales—The people don't lie!—while visual artists, who might not sell what they make to even one person, can work at the limits of their art without the overt burden of audience pleasure (read: Snickers and Cheez Doodles) in mind, it seems better to be pleased that this book is back in the hands of people who might read it for themselves. This is what matters. It is not difficult, unnecessarily challenging, minor, or needlessly cerebral. *Motorman* is a central work, pulsing with mythology, created by a craftsman of language who was seemingly channeling the history of narrative when he wrote it. It is a book about the future that comes from the past, and we are caught in its amazing middle.

If we had to label it, *Motorman* might be called apathy noir, a gasless detective story minus the detective, set inside a hollowed-out egg, with flashlight shadows roving the shell. The inventions and fabulations—the double suns, the fake years—seem to flow from Ohle's left hand, which is to say that his bursts of oddity are never showcased, but rather incidental and down-played, as if they might not really be happening, and this distinguishes him from many concept-driven sci-fi writers who are eager to lacquer their imaginations to a full gloss and create a museum spectacle of their concepts.

At the level of story, *Motorman* is a digressive escape narrative, with a vaguely persecuted main character of the sort one might find in Kafka. But while Kafka's bureaucratic settings were clinical, grey, and typically consonant with architectural reality, Ohle has embel-lished his world with impossible weather, illogical time structures, and enhanced surveillance powers, including bursts of craziness and color that might have embarrassed poor Kafka. It's fitting that Ohle quotes Escher, whose fabulist, escape-free structures are much like what Moldenke, *Motorman*'s hero, discovers as he travels through a territory called "the bottoms." Escher created images that appear logical and coher-ent on paper, but could not exist in three dimensions. They perfectly assert the purity of imagined space, the intractability of what can be conceived. They argue that the third dimension should be called "disappointment." Ohle, too, is expert at contriving logical veracity for the most impossible scenarios. His delivery is droll and often bloodless, from the side of his mouth, and thus the strange happenings of his story appear strangely true. Adjectives are anathema to Ohle. Precision and clarity are all. He is mathematical and concise in his descriptions, never wasting a word. And he favors the short, one-sentence paragraph.

Which has a way of knocking you over the head, creating propulsion into even the most strangely decorated narrative tunnels.

The narrative tunnels which, when you turn the page, you will enter for yourself.

To read *Motorman* now is to encounter proof that a book can be both emotional and eccentric, smeared with humanity and artistically ambitious, messy with grief and dazzling with spectacle. Do not think, however, that you are entirely protected reading it, although I can mostly vouchsafe about the claims of cindering. At this time, chances are fairly good that you will not burn.

Now you're on your own.

Ben Marcus   2004

For Beverly, Alice, and Ed Wolfe

Bricks are usually rectangular, because in that way they are most suitable for building the vertical walls of our houses. But anyone who has had to do with the stacking of stones of a non-cubic type will be well aware of other possibilities. For instance, one can make use of tetrahedrons alternating with octahedrons. They are not practicable for human beings to build with, because they make neither vertical walls nor horizontal floor. However, when this building is filled with water, flatworms can swim in it.
–M.C. Escher

MOTORMAN

1]

Moldenke would remain.

As a child they kept him in a crumbling house, a building with structural moans, whose eaves cracked in summer heat and gathered winter ice.

At that point Moldenke's chest held two lungs and a single heart.

He experienced a shortened boyhood, a small degree of youth and carelessness.

Most phenomena puzzled him and sent him on aimless walks among the leafless ether trees. He would fix on his goggles, his gauze pad, and study the flying birds, see them casting frightened earthward glances.

He would press his face against the pane of his bedroom lookout as spring fell and wait for the greenbird. The greenbird would circle a dying ether, peck spirals on its dry trunk. Moldenke would fold himself into a chair and watch the greenbird work, writing down its habits, behaviors, and essences:

Rapid pecking followed by pauses. Long, agile tongue coated with a jellylike substance, good for rooting in tree trunks for larvae and etcetera. When the tongue is retracted it apparently wraps about the brain.

Things were loose in those days for Moldenke. He was free and new green, bright suns behind him, spirals ahead.

2]

When his mind wandered it took him to a sunchoked acre of grasses and weed where a snow of pollen lay yellow on the ground, a place like a rotunda, obviously complete, although nothing suggested architecture. There was no apparent ceiling and no visible dome.

Warm winds would lap at his stringy hair arrangement. He would feel no pulse, faint metabolism, conscious only of the hum and flow. He would recall what Doctor Burnheart had said to him on one occasion: "Take wing, Moldenke. Life is flight if you choose to ride the updrafts."

He would circle the acre in pollen silence with his better ear open. The silence would give way to a labored breathing, the sound of a single lung in difficulty. Then, on a cue from no visible source, something with mudded claws would spit clots from surrounding bushes. Moldenke would imagine himself turning away, his chin on his chest, one hand in a pocket.

The Moldenke mind was airy, like a dirigible loosed from its tethers.

3]

He felt something without form, something edgeless, rushing at him from the direction of eastern light. He pressed his nose against a lookout, saw a pattern coming together at the horizon of city and sky. He crabbed backwardly up the false stairwell and crouched in a blind spot. "Is that you, Bunce? Mr. Bunce?"

It moved through his room, the visitor, touching things to its nose and snorting, and sat in Moldenke's chair.

Moldenke turned on a light, "Yes?"

The visitor stood and approached him, opening its ear valve to relieve pressure. "You should stay in the chair now, Moldenke. I will remain in the hallway and watch your door. It is a pleasure to know you."

4]

The phone rang. Moldenke picked up the speaker:

"Hello?"

"Yes, hello." It seemed a genuine voice. "Is this Moldenke?"

"Yes, it is."

"Well, well...Moldenke?"

"Yes, who is this?"

"Never mind that. By the way, are you leaning against a wall?"

"No."

"Would you mind?"

"No, I wouldn't."

"Then please lean."

"The phone is in the middle of the room. I can't."

"Good, try squatting."

Moldenke squatted. "There. Now, who's calling?"

"Never mind that, jocko. You know who this is."

"Mr. Bunce?"

"Exactly correct, Mr. Moldenke. Old friend Bunce. What say we halt these amenities and face the grit? I have a reason for calling you, jocko. A number of reasons in fact; one particular is a pressing little matter of tapes. You might say I called to talk tape. That would be sufficient."

"I'm not playing, Bunce."

"He's not playing, he says."

'That's right."

"I warn you not to fiddle, Moldenke. This is a business call and I'm speaking on a business phone."

Moldenke felt floor through his soft, catkin slippers, was conscious of trapped gas within his pajamas, imagined a raincoat under his skin, and an indoor rain.

"We're talking dumps, Moldenke. Don't give me gas. I have some tapes here that may be of major importance to you, all nicely packaged and locked in my kitty-box."

Moldenke hung up.

6

5]

Dear Moldenke,

    I think of you often these days. How are things in the cities? I wish you could be with me in this country air. Yes, Moldenke. *Air*. You should be breathing it occasionally, if not constantly. After all, you're the one with the problem heart.

    My special regards, as ever,
    Doctor Burnheart

6]

She would say, "Play the Buxtehude, Moldenke. I enjoy the chills it gives me." She would close the door behind herself and leave him alone in the piano room with its pots of ivy and ant-traps.

    He would begin the Buxtehude on the cold keyboard. In the bedroom she would listen through a wall.

    He would play the Buxtehude until ants crawled along his fingers and assembled on his sleeves.

    He would then walk to the kitchen, carrying his hands like packages, and scrape the ants into a teaboil. Roberta would emerge from the bedroom, stand in the doorway in her flannel. Moldenke would turn from the tea boil and smile, his old silver tooth throwing out a rod of light.

    Roberta would say, "Tea?"

    Moldenke would add mock sugar. "Yes, would you like a cup?"

She would always have a cup. She would say, "As always."

Moldenke would have his with potato milk, she without.

7]

When he was a boy, a student, whenever he loaned out a book it would come back with nosewipes in the margins and down the spine.

8]

He put the speaker to his better ear and listened for a dial tone. There was static, someone pouring rice from bowl to bowl.

He fixed the speaker in its cradle and went to his lookout. Buildings, vehicles, something above suggesting sky.

Two suns up, a bright day.

American hearts beating in the street.

9]

Over the seasons Moldenke's faith diminished. If he opened a spigot and got water, no matter how clouded or sour, he was gratified, as though he no longer expected it, although he loved water as nearly as he loved anything. That was the way with Moldenke, a brightly burning candle with a shortened wick, destined to burn low and give off gas.

10]

The phone rang. Moldenke answered:

"Hello?"

"May I speak to Mr. Moldenke?"

"This is Mr. Moldenke speaking. Who's calling?"

"Bunce here, Moldenke. Serious up a minute, please. No fooling around. I don't like the way you hung up on me last call. I never like to see a hang-up. It shows me you're not as interested as you should be, not as engaged as you might be. What's the trouble? Would you like me to put my forearm up your very delicate chuff pipe and pop your spleen like a cherry, or run my thumbnail down your inner spine, assuming you have one? Is that the sort of thing you want? Bunce doesn't cater to the meek, my friend. Remember *that* even if you forget all else. Remember that much. Open the good ear, jocko. Listen to me. We have the tapes."

"You have the tapes," Moldenke said. "What tapes?"

"What tapes, he says."

"Yes, Bunce. What tapes?"

"Tapes, friend. Tapes! Things said about you in your absence. Yourself as others see you. The works. We have it all. The whole Moldenke. If you ever have a yen to listen to a few of the tapes, give me a call. The number is 555-333-555333-555-333. I'll be around. Give me a ring sometime. We'll have lunch, slug down a few pinebrews, and talk things over. Put all our bags on the table, if you know what I mean. Are you with me, Moldenke? Can you follow me?"

Moldenke again hung up.

11]

He opened the book to a random page, let his finger float to a random line and read: *In 1856 Claude Bernard noted the appearance of cloudy lymph in the duodenum near the entrance of the bile duct.* He read no further.

12]

He dialed in a station on the radio and got a weather report:

Cloudy, freezing in the outskirts, cold tonight, colder tomorrow, warming Thursday and Friday, cooling off by Saturday, sleet by Sunday, double suns on Monday, and so on, according to the everyday charts, indicating a possible trend—warm, cool, cooler, etcetera, chance of light-to-heavy blister snow, probable drizzle washing out the artificial month, gas breaks at Amarillo, Great Chicago, and Texaco City, no moons tonight, shelter animals if necessary, please stay tuned...

13]

He dialed 555-333-555333-555-333, an obvious woman answered the first ring:

"Chelsea Fish Pavilion."

"Excuse me," Moldenke said. "I may have misdialed. My apologies."

"Sir, what number did you call?"

"I don't remember. What number did I reach?"

"The Chelsea Fish, 555-333—"

"Thank you, miss. The number sounds familiar, although I don't think—"

"May 1 help you, sir?"

"I don't know, miss. Is there by any odd chance some-one in the establishment by the name of Bunce?"

"Yes, sir. The Manager, Mr. Bunce. Would you like me to connect you with him?"

"No, miss. I already am. Thank you. And, miss?"

"Yes, sir?"

"Is he what you call the boss?"

"Yes, sir. He is."

"I see. Well, thanks, miss. I was only verifying the number. I didn't have anything to talk about. I may come in and buy a few nice fish sometime."

"We don't have any, sir. I'm sorry."

"Oh?"

"Goodbye, sir."

"Goodbye, miss."

14]

He went to his kitty-file and took out a Burnheart letter:

11

Dear Moldenke,

Yesterday I had a productive visit with my friend Eagleman of Atmospheric Sciences. He was full of his ensiform work with *oecanthus* and it took him several cigars to get it all on the table, as it were.

One question, Dinky: how are the polyps?
Cordially yours,
Doc Burnheart

P.S. Have you seen Eagleman's moon?

15]

After the mock War was apparently over, the army let Moldenke go. He found work as a bloodboy in a gauze mill outside Texaco City, a klick or two from the L.A. limits. He started low and remained there, sure that safety embraced felicity on a mattress of obscurity. He knew that vertical activity invited dazzling exposure, and that to seek is to be sucked. He recognized loneliness as the mother of virtues and sat in her lap whenever he could. He practiced linear existence and sidewise movement, preferring the turtle to the crane, the saucer to the lamp. He enjoyed the downstairs and chafed at going up. All of this, despite what his mother had told him: "Sonny," she had said, a circle of rouge on each of her cheeks, her eyes like basement windows. "Son," she said, "I want you to always have a job to go to, no matter what it is or where it is or what it involves. What matters is whether or not it lets you go up."

16]

The lights went out. The radio died. Moldenke went to the lookout. Both suns were up, and clouded over. It was dark enough to be close to noons, although he didn't have a clockpiece anywhere. The second double Sunday in an artificial month.

He opened his refrigerator and found a cockroach at the lettuce. Something scratched in the eggs.

The juice was off. He would call the Power Co-op.

17]

The phone rang.

Moldenke answered.

"Hello?"

"Am I speaking with Moldenke?"

"Yes. Bunce? Bunce, my lights are off."

"His lights are off, he says."

"And the radio, and the refrigerator. What about my weather reports? I'm worried. The wind is dying. What about those things, Bunce?"

"Moldenke fiddles on. The lights are off, the wind is dying. Moldenke, if we were back-to-back we'd tangle asses."

"The heat grille went off also. I should add that. I'm getting colder."

"Hey, pal, listen to this: I'm taking you out of the M's and putting you at the top of the A's, smack at the head of my list. Here it is, jock: From now on, only one outgoing call per day, two incoming, all monitored. Consider benefits and privileges terminated, and don't leave your room until I say so. I don't *necessarily* want blood, but don't rule it out. Read a few magazines. No moving around. Pick a chair you like and stay with it. No changing. I'll have your food sent up. What do you think this is, Moldenke? A nightflying outfit? Don't be so casual about it, boy. How would you like to spend an hour in the hot room? I want seriousness from you. Remember, if you don't ease up, you might get plugged."

"What are you doing, Bunce?"

"What am I doing, he says."

"Why the hot room threat, why the sudden restrictions? If this is a mistake I'll forgive it right now, but if it's a josh I don't know what I'll do. Is it a mistake? A josh? A shuck?"

"No. Perfectly serious. I want your close attention, Moldenke. You're in my hands."

"No, Bunce. I decline. I'm hanging up now; maybe I'll run the movie backward a few frames, and the phone won't ring."

"Can the tricks, boy."

"I don't believe this, Bunce. I need proof, some sign."

"You want proof?"

"I want a sign."

"All right, boy. A sign. Stand there awhile and then go to the lookout."

Moldenke waited, went to the lookout, watched an amber cocacola mist fade into a yellow drizzle. Proof? He scanned two horizons, surveyed the streets.

Nothing. No sign. Pigeons in eaves across the way. No k-vehicles. The Health Truck passed.

An ant crawled over Moldenke's shoe and went up a wall.

Something climbed from shelf to shelf in the refrigerator.

A dull hissing, distant, then close. He spun in the darkness, saw its eyelike headlight, heard the jelly slosh.

18]

A genuine month before this, Moldenke had been driving his k-rambler along a white boulevard curving around a stadium. At a certain point on the curve he saw a couple, man and woman. The woman knelt over the gutter, favoring her stomach, her face a shade of purple. Moldenke stopped. The man, tobacco-stained and scholarly, asked if Moldenke would be so kind as to give them a ride to a drugstore for a tin of "shark" tablets, for the woman's illness.

They lifted her onto the back seat and drove on down the wide boulevard, Moldenke beginning to have some doubts about the couple. The woman grunted in the back and gave off an odor.

"Shark tablets?" Moldenke questioned.

The man nodded and agreed.

"For the wife?" Moldenke questioned again.

The man said, "Yez," with a "z," a mannerism Moldenke never enjoyed.

He saw a slight movement over the man's eye. He looked. An eyebrow dangled over the eye, parts of the face flaking down the suit.

He took out a cigar, testing.

"No flames, pliz!" He turned the face toward Moldenke.

Moldenke held out his cigar lighter, his thumb on the flint. "Why not?" He turned the flint slowly, the car filling with gas.

The moustache slid down the tie. Above the paper collar the plastic had begun to curl. Now Moldenke was sure—a pair of jellyheads working the streets. He shouldn't have picked them up, but he had. He would do what Burnheart had told him to do on a number of occasions; he would open them up.

He gunned the k-rambler and drove toward the bottoms. Traffic thinned and ended. Civilization gave way to a marshland, veined with treeless ridges. At every klick-marker a blind road turned into the bottoms. He picked one and drove along slush ruts until they ended, stopped, and turned off the motor.

He looked at the rubber face. "Are you a pair of Bunce's jellyheads?"

In the back the woman sat up, said nothing. Most of the man's features had broken loose and tumbled down to the seat and floor. The head, without makeup, a gray balloon, something sloshing inside it.

"I asked if you were on Bunce's payroll." He turned the flint faster.

They chose silence.

"Okay," Moldenke said. "Then get out of the car and take your medicine. I've got you fair. Don't resist me."

They climbed out. Moldenke exposed his letter opener.

"You first." The man came forward. "Bend over." The man bowed. With the letter opener, Moldenke opened a small hole in the back of the neck, enough for two fingers. He put a thumb and a forefinger in and widened the hole, a clear jelly spilling out, down his trenchpants. The air smelled of laboratories. He did the woman, her jelly more clouded, her rubber skull a little thicker than the professor's had been.

In the morning, with two suns behind him like stray moons, he examined his vehicle. The odor of laboratories was there, although faint. In the back seat the same jelly substance, studded with nibs, as though the woman had eaten peanuts, had washed across the upholstery.

19]

There was a knock at the door, either soft hands or gloved fingers. The meal was there from Bunce, on a tray in the hall, on the floor. The first meal from Bunce. He was hungry. He took the tray inside and ate. The tray had three hollows: catmeat filled one, boiled crickets filled the second, and a chunk of stale pinebread with ant sauce filled the third.

20]

A letter came from Burnheart:

Dear Moldenke,
    Cheer up. Things are approaching the jell.
Nothing is final as yet, but we are working it
through. Eagleman sends his regards. He's a good
man to know. We should consider ourselves among
the fortunate few. What would a winter night be like
without Eagleman's moon? Tell me that. Crowded
almost out now with government moons, but still the
brightest light in the sky. We have no one to thank
for Eagleman except...Eagleman.
    This letter has a purpose. Enclosed, please find
a simple, one-part questionnaire. Fill it out and get
it back to me as soon as you can. We can't move an
inch without the information.
    Cordial greetings,
    Burnheart

The questionnaire:

You are shad fishing in a plainly marked mu-
nicipal water tub, or (2) you chance by a swollen
river. The fog log, you remember from the radio
weather, is at 77. The ambient light is dim, or (2)
very bright. As you gaze over the water's surface
you see what appears to be the corpse of a dray
horse, bridled even in death, with sodden frag-
ments of the dray still attached. No moons are
up, or (2) two moons are up, or (3) the sun is
simply down, or (4) more than one sun is down.
You rise up to your feet and take another look.
Caution: It may not be a horse at all. *Additional
Caution*: If it is a horse it is either bloated, or (2)
there is a plate-sized hole in its belly to relieve
the pressures of rot. The animal floats closer to
the breakwater, now clearly in danger of rubbing
barnacles. Your hearts leap up. Your spleen puff.
WHAT NOW? (See below)

(USE THIS SPACE)

_____

_____

_____

19

He called the Power Co-op:

"Good afternoon, sir. Power Co-op. May I help you this afternoon, sir?" The voice was feminine, high pitched, a refined whistle.

Moldenke was puzzled. Something already wasn't exactly right. "Miss, how did you know I was male?"

"Sir?"

"I wanted to know how it was that you knew I was a 'sir,' instead of a 'miss,' or a 'little boy,' or something like that."

"Sir?"

"That's right. You pinned it down as soon as you answered. I hadn't even opened my mouth. But you knew I was male. I wanted to know how you knew. That's all."

"Sir? Didn't you say your name? You said something."

"No, ma'am. Nothing. Was it my breathing? A man's breathing is a touch huskier than a woman's, or a child's, is that the trick?"

"No, sir. Please excuse my enthusiasm. It's my first day on the job, sir. If I've made an error, then we apologize. We beg your pardon."

"Fine, that's fine, miss. Now, what I called about is my electricity. It suddenly went off a while back. No radio, no weather reports, no heat, nothing. I need some service out here."

"Certainly, Mr. Moldenke. We'll do what we can to—"

"Miss?"

"Sir?"

"Now I'm more than a little bit puzzled. First there was the 'sir.' Now you give me a clean, crisp, *Mr. Moldenke*, as though I had actually told you my name. I haven't mentioned the name yet, have I, miss?"

"Yes, sir. You did...you must have. Didn't you?"

"No, ma'am. I haven't. I'm sure of it. Let me speak to the supervisor."

"Please, sir. We apologize. This is my first day."

"Don't worry, miss. You'll keep the job. You're very good at it, but a little too fast for me. Your supervisor, please."

"Sir, he's not in the building at the moment."

"Does he have a supervisor?"

"Yes, sir."

"Then I'll speak to him. Connect me with him."

"Yes, sir. That would be Mr. Bunce. Just a moment."

"Miss?"

"Sir?"

"Never mind. Cancel the whole thing. Goodbye."

"Sir?"

The only outgoing, thrown to the winds.

22]

Moldenke sat henlike in his chair, brooding in the dark, chewing a stonepick. The door opened halfway, showing an obelisk of hall light, and Burnheart came in, striking matches.

"Burnheart? Is that you, Burnheart?"

"Moldenke?" He held the match an inch from Moldenke's chin. "Why do you live like this, Moldenke? You get more like a rat every season. What do they pay you to live here? I smell urine. Where's the straw?" The match went out. He struck another one, moving it up and down, looking at the whole Moldenke.

"Burnheart. I'm happy to see you. Sit down somewhere. Let's talk. I thought you were in the country with Eagleman."

"I was. I was in the country. However, now I'm in the city. I move with my moods. My mood said city, and here I am, a toad in the frog pond, as they say. Why am I striking matches like this? Turn on the lights."

"I can't. They're off. That's one of the things I wanted to talk to you about."

"What do I know about practical electricity? It's not my field. What could I say?"

"No no. I'm concerned about why they're off, not that they're off. I think it's Bunce."

"Bunce?"

"You know the man?"

"Bunce. Yes, I know Bunce...You must have a candle around. Is there a candle, Moldenke? Some kind of light source?"

"I'm afraid not. Burnheart, tell me what to do. I don't know of anyone else who can advise me. What should I do about Bunce?"

"What a season this has been, Moldenke. What a season. My old heart won't stand another one like it. So many loads in the old gun and so on. I sometimes consider retiring, quitting the whole thing. Of course, someone always steps in and reminds me that I have nothing to retire from. So I never do. I continue slaving and worrying over nothing substantial. I'm plumb tired. The system is wearing out. I plan to get back to the country as fast as I can. Sometimes, there, I hear the chirp of a snipe, and that reminds me that I'm still alive. What does it all matter?"

"Sit down, Burnheart. Talk."

"Where, Moldenke? Are there chairs in a rat's den? Where shall I sit?" Moldenke occupied the only chair.

"Take this chair."

"No, Moldenke. You stay there. You need the rest. You're still young. Rest while you can. There's nothing ahead but rattles." Another match went out. "Some light is better than none. We'll smoke cigars." Burnheart lit two blue cigars with his last match and gave one to Moldenke. "Here, Moldenke. Puff hard and constantly. We'll get close to one another and puff rapidly." Burnheart knelt, squaring his height with Moldenke's. Moldenke remained in the chair. They studied one another in the wavering orange swells of light, through smoke and running eyes.

"Burnheart, I may have broken an unwritten rule of some kind. I'm not sure."

"Well, then. If *you're* not sure, how can *I* be sure? How can we talk about it? Tell me more, Dinky."

"I think I opened up a couple of Bunce's jellyheads. But I'm not sure."

"You're not sure?"

23

"No, I had been chewing stonepicks. I was seeing and feeling through cotton. I'm not certain."

"I've told you about stonepicks. Say I haven't."

"You have."

"You had one in your mouth when I came in. Say you didn't."

"I didn't."

"So you opened a pair of jellies?"

"Yes, *maybe* I did. The recollection is full of holes."

"But there is a recollection?"

"Yes, I woke up with it. It was strong. I checked my clothes, my vehicle. There was definitely jelly, and those nibs."

"What did you do it with?"

"I may have done it with my letter opener."

"May I see it?" Moldenke gave him the letter opener, a simple chrome affair with swirls. He smelled it, touched it, gave it back. The cigars were halfway done. "I'd say you did it, or someone did it with your letter opener, wearing your clothes, and driving your vehicle. One or the other. I'm afraid I don't know what to say, Dinky. Bunce has a great deal of pull."

"Help me, Burnheart."

"I don't know, Moldenke. I just don't know. All I can do is be your friend. I'm only a scientist. I have my limits."

"Should I run?"

"I'd sit still for a while."

"What should I do?"

"I'd do nothing for a while."

They blinked, coughed. The cigars wore down. Burnheart went to the lookout. "There it is. The city. The rooftops of the city. Back in the city again. My mood is changing sooner than I expected it would. I'll have to head back toward the country."

"Burnheart. Stay longer."

"No. I have experiments to run, rats and rabbits to feed. You know the game."

"Are you leaving now?"

"Yes. I only came to bring you a letter I'd written and forgot to mail. I thought I'd deliver it personally as long as I was in the city. It may be the last time I'm here. My city moods come less and less often these days, and this one feels final." He gave Moldenke a letter. "It may be a little out of date, as they say."

"I'll read it anyway."

"Well, Dink. I'll be seeing you. If you need my advice about anything, give me a call. Don't flounder around uncertain about things. Call me."

"Are we friends, Burnheart?"

"Straight on, Dink. Double-clutching heart-mates. I'll see you around." He left, closed the door softly behind him.

23]

He dialed 555-333-555333-555-333.

"Fernberg's Clock & Hock, Bunce on the line."

"Mr. Bunce?"

"Yes?"

25

"I thought I'd call and sort of feel things out."

"Who is this?"

"Moldenke."

"Oh, Moldenke. I didn't recognize the voice. Throat polyps, is that it? You shouldn't be breathing so much, boy. Wear the gauze pads. Wear the gauze pads. Why do you think we give them to you? What do you want? I'm a busy man this season."

"Like I said before, I thought I'd call and sort of—"

"I heard it the first time. Explain yourself."

"Well, there really isn't too much in the way of things to explain, Mr. Bunce. I suppose, if you have to say something, say I'm testing. Throwing out my bait."

"Don't tell me what to say."

"I didn't."

"Don't."

"I won't."

"The future lies ahead of us, boy, hanging there like a thunderstorm. Make yourself a shelter. Quit gassing, stop your aimless pissing-off. Collect things. Pull your coats tight. Get ready."

"Mr. Bunce?"

"Yes?"

"Suppose, in a few minutes from now, suppose I get up from this chair and walk to the door, open the door, step into the hall, walk down the stairs, through the main gate, and out into the street. What then?"

"Don't bother, champ. You won't get past the open door part. I've got a man in the hall. You won't make it. Stay with the chair."

"I'm beginning to itch."

"He's beginning to itch."

"Sores on the underthigh."

"Sores on the underthigh, he says."

"I'm not very comfortable with these restrictions."

"He's not very comfortable. Moldenke! You gutted two of my very best street workers. You expect comfort, you expect to be left alone? Moldenke?"

"What?"

"Look at the palm of your left hand."

"I can't. The lights are out."

"Wait a second. I'll turn them on for a minute." The lights flickered and went on. Moldenke stood up, legs stiff, bloodless. He sat back down. The refrigerator hummed. The radio went on, the heater grille twittered like a redbird. Feet shuffled on the carpet in the hall. Somewhere in the building unit a toilet flushed.

"Did you do that, Bunce? Did you make the lights go on? Is my electricity somehow flowing through the Fernberg Clock & Hock?"

"Look at the left palm, Moldenke." He looked at the palm.

"Okay, Bunce. I'm looking. Now what?"

"Are you looking at it closely?"

"As close as I can under the circumstances."

"What are the circumstances?"

"Mucus collecting in one of the eyes. It's all but cemented shut."

"Wear the goggles, boy. Why do you think we give you goggles? Now, hold the palm up there and look twice as hard." Moldenke did that. "Are you looking hard enough?"

"I'm looking. I'm looking."

"Pay attention to surface conditions, qualities of the skin, stuff like that."

Moldenke studied the palm. The lights surged, the radio went louder. Outside, the wind picked up. The door of the refrigerator opened and swung back on its hinges. A weather report came on the radio:

Possible dry storms in the bottoms area, reports not confirmed, estimates of high winds, gauzemen working overshifts, nothing official, stay tuned, remain calm...

"Did you hear that, Bunce?"

"Yes, I heard it. It was a good one. I liked it. What about the palm? Have you looked at it sufficiently?"

"Yes, I think so."

"Good. Now, look at the pocket on the hip matching that palm you just looked at so intently." Moldenke looked at the left pocket, examined it.

"Examine the pocket, Moldenke."

"I am. I am." He saw grease, hanging strings, and dirt.

"Good. Tell me what you see." Moldenke told him what he had seen. "Fine. Look at the palm again." He looked at the palm again. "Have you looked?"

"Yes."

"Perfect. Now, put the palm in the pocket, along with the hand." He put the hand in his pocket, along with the palm. "Is it in there good?"

"Yes. It's not so easy sitting down."

"Good enough. Now, take it out." He took it out. "Is it out?"

"Yes. It's out."

"Excellent, boy. Now, tell me what you've learned from this."

"I suppose I've learned that the palm remains while the pocket wears away. Skin regenerates, cloth is a one-way business. Something like that. I learned something along those lines. Am I right?"

"Close enough, close enough. Hah! And they call old Burnheart a great scientist. I wonder about his pupil. Moldenke, you're a clever boy. Pure reason, almost untainted, white light, etcetera. I would probably love you, Moldenke, if times were right. I'd strap on my artificial vagina for you. We could slug a few pinebrews and watch some football. If things were only a little tighter, or a great deal looser than they are, who knows? Sure, I wear a smear of rouge. Sure, I've dug potatoes out of garbage hills. Sure, I've played my share of football. And what does it come to? A throat full of polyps and a set of false eyes. Moldenke, you're sliding downward. I am not your friend. The test is over."

24]

He read the letter Burnheart had left:

Dear Friend Moldenke,
   Some years back, as I gather, the government
phased out the postal cats. Heretofore, as you may
be aware, the government was actually paying
them 10 chit a paper week to eat the rats and other
rodents that were eating the mail, a kind of twisted
food-chain deal. That plan went along nicely for a
time, until some jellyhead in some post office hole
decided that further rules were needed in order
to stem the tide of profiteering, slave-holding, and
poison-running, which rose among the cats. These
rules were known as the Private Bag Ordinances
(the P.B.O.'s), and they generally held that the rats
of a given mail bag were the property, the *private* and
exclusive property of the cat who could daily stalk
the area of the bag. Naturally, this served only to
increase the dominance of the stronger cats over the
weaker cats, as you might expect. Not surprisingly,
the weaker cats lobbied for ordinances declaring
that all bags must be watched equally and that all
proceeds should be divided accordingly.
   Enough of this, Moldenke. I'm off to the
greenhouse.
   See you in the city.
   As always,
   Burnheart

25]

Burnheart called:
    "Moldenke?"
    "Burnheart?"
    "Yes, speaking. Dink? One question: Why hasn't he thought of unplugging the phone?"
    "The phone? The telephone? My telephone?"
    "Right. Why not?"
    "I don't know. I hadn't thought of it either."
    "Wrong, Dink. He's thought of it. He's considered it. A few years back I might have said he was capable of oversights, but not now. The most we can hope for now is chance and accident. Are you with me? Together, Dink. Me and you. We'll roll him like a pill in our fingers. Say, Dink? Have you noted my high mood?"
    "Yes. You seem up. Upper than you were the last I saw you."
    "Naturally. I'm back in the country. One sniff of the peat and I'm mysteriously restored. Energy surges again. Now and again we toss a bucket of crabs out to the hogs. The hogs live among the pilings under the house. You've never seen this place, have you? That will have to be fixed. The country is almost alive with occasional activity. The other day I was sitting on a gum stump watching an unusual sort of insect crawl up a dead brush plant. A very colorful bug, stripes, crescents, long, fernlike antennae. You know the sort, Moldenke?"
    "Sure I know. The decorator bug."

"Yes, of course. The decorator bug. When he reached the top of a branch he attached himself by the hinder legs and began unfurling himself. Membranes fanned out, wings turned and adjusted themselves. And there he was, a flower. Later, other decorator bugs came along and settled in place—buds, leaves, even a mock wasp. It was a natural gas, Moldenke. You'd never see that in the city, would you?"

"I guess not."

"Then come to the country. Be with me and Eagleman."

"Bunce says no moving. How would I get there?"

"Did I say we were friends?"

"Sure, but what if—"

"We'll have him picking his nose in the cold room. I'm convinced he has flaws. The only weapon he has is you, Moldenke. Follow what I say?"

"Yeah, but what should I do?"

"Test him."

"Well, I already tried one test and it didn't—"

"Never mind. I'll design the tests. All you have to do is execute them. Eagleman is with us. Nobody can cipher better than Eagleman. He'll carry us through this affair even if you don't. Moldenke, place yourself at our disposal. Will you do that? Remember who installed your hearts? I've held your old heart in my fingers. How close can two people get? You've already trusted me with your heart. How about a little surrender, Dink? Give us yourself."

"Sure, why not? When do you want me? Will you come and get me?"

"No."

"Can I drive out in my k-ram—"

"No. No. Wait awhile. I'll think about it, talk to Eagleman. I'll call you back tomorrow with a test. We'll spring a test on him tomorrow. Would you like to say anything?"

"No... Except one thing. It may not be important."

"Everything is. What is it?"

"I haven't flushed the water dump in more than a week."

"Why not?"

"There hasn't been a need to."

"You're being oblique, Moldenke. Does that mean you haven't taken a dump in that long a time?"

"Yes. That long."

"That's a long time, Dink. In a day or two you'll be coughing it up. Not good for the hearts. A constipated system is a threat to the flow. Lie on the left side and press the abdomen. Have an old fashioned enema. We can't be running subtle tests with full intestines. Tell me, are you drinking liquids?"

"No. I don't have any. Somebody turned off the water, too. Probably Bunce."

"Tell me, are you passing gas?"

"Seldom. A cold sputter or two every other day."

"You've got the dry poots. Get on it. I'll ring you tomorrow. I'll have a test ready. Have a fair day."

33

In the morning two suns came up, brightening the room, yellowing the walls. He could see. He stood up and fell forward on elbows and a knee. Someone with a hammer could have driven a nail in his back. His feelings were gone. He was stung. He would have tried to move his legs had he been able even to imagine them. He thought of Burnheart. He imagined Burnheart. He pulled himself along the rug and up the bedside, turning his face to the lookout, to the suns. He sat on the bed, opened his shirts, gave his hairless chest to the light. He pressed the abdomen, formed fists and beat pain into his legs. A rush of blood, circulation, a stirring of deep nerves, feeling.

A greenbird flew to the lip of the lookout, grappled for footing, stunned, flapping off feathers, fell backward, down, streetward.

A city chicken cockled.

He would keep busy. He would find his lighter, the flints, the bottle of k-fuel. He would drag his kitty-file closer to the chair. He would exercise. He would write Burnheart a letter. Generally, he would move. He wouldn't remain seated any longer.

He sat on the water dump and wrote:

Dear Burny,

I'm not sure you can help me out of this unless you know me better than you do. How well do you actually know me? You sometimes refer to me as

Dink, or Dinky, my school name, which is a nice, familiar thing to do. But what does it amount to when you consider all the other things about me you don't know? I realize it seems insignificant. But it only seems that way. It really isn't. It is. It *is* significant. You can be assured that Bunce knows more than my school name. Burnheart, you should be more aware of me. You should know every lonely detail, everything, the whole Moldenke. For example: What did I do when I wandered away from the gauze mill? Did I take a job shrimping? If not, why so? Do you know that? You should. Bunce does. He could account for every moment. He has tapes, and I wouldn't be surprised if he also had films. Burnheart, please don't take this letter as an attempt at criticism, which is the most distant thing from my mind these days. No, it isn't that at all. It must be something else. Unfortunately, I don't know what. I enjoyed seeing you on your trip to the city and I look forward to being with you and Eagleman in the country. I've kept a picture of you on the wall. I've always looked up to you. If you ever came to me and said, "Rub something," I'd rub it without a second thought. I've copied your signature too many times. I've read the letters thin. You send me your throwaway coats and I manage to need them. I consider it an honor to wear them. How many of your test tubes have I washed? Ten thousand? How many solutions have I cooked on your k-flame? I've used you as a laxative and a lubricant both.

Still, I see you as a stranger. Burnheart, help me.
I'm getting along badly. Send me a woman. I need
a woman. This morning the last scab peeled off
the crank. I'm ready; although I'm afraid I have no
feeling.
    Yours,
    I surrender,
    Moldenke

He balled the letter and threw it in the water
dump.
    The suns had gone above the building. The room
dimmed. Had there been water he would have bathed.
He opened the spigot, testing, got sour air and pipe
vibes. He wouldn't bathe and go to bed. He hadn't
dumped.
    He closed the dead refrigerator door. It opened
again, back on its hinges. He had startled something.
It flew past his shoulder, tipping his ear, fluttering into
the bed springs.
    He would pass time reading Burnheart letters. He
found the lighter, loaded in a new flint, filled the tank
with k-fuel, sparked it, and read by its light.

Dear Moldenke,
    You remind me of the tripodero. You know the
tripodero? A small creature of the Newer England
woods? I'm not certain whether it has met extinction
or not as yet. But that doesn't matter. We have
records of him, specimens. He'd race along the

hedgerows, churning up the turf, always sensitive to danger on the other side. If he ever suspected it, why, he'd rise up on those three telescoping legs of his and have a look. A marvelous mammal, the tripodero. I wonder whether he's still alive?

Your Instructor,
Doctor Burnheart

The lighter grew hot in Moldenke's hands. The room cooled.

He read another letter, a short letter attached to the one he had just read:

Dear Dink,

If you sense danger, rise up. I'll be over the hedge.

Be cautious,
Burnheart

He chewed a stonepick and watched the moons come up, fell asleep in his chair.

27]

She came to him as a stranger in the Tropical Garden. He first saw her figure in the banana leaves. He spaded earth ceremoniously and watched her from the corner of his eye. She tossed a banana flower at his foot and warmed him with a flow of spirit and a smile. He raised his trowel and indicated the greenhouse.

They walked among the rows of succulents, pressing thick leaves between their fingers. She broke open the stalk of an ice plant, drew a circle on his forehead with its juices, made an *x* inside the circle. The space around them fell into silent patterns.

She lifted her Indian dress and dipped a foot in the frog pool.

Two suns were up.

She said her name was Cock Roberta.

28]

The phone rang. It was Burnheart:

"Still constipated?"

"Yes. I tried last night. Nothing would move."

"Then we'll have to go full, that's all. Nothing ever works exactly right. Luckily, you don't often get to eat. You'll be needing some liquids, though. I have a test ready. Let's get this thing going. When you get here I'll personally give you an enema. Are you ready for the test?"

"Sure. What should I do?"

"Simple. Go to the door, open it, step into the hall, walk to the stairway, make it down the stairs, through the main gate, and into the street. If you get that far, head south for the country. Eagleman and I will be waiting for you with a soft bed and solid food. Come."

"I can't. Bunce has a man in the hall."

"Ignore the man. He isn't there, even if it seems like he is. I know Bunce's games."

"I hear the feet shuffling out there, inflations, de-flations. Bunce has a jellyhead out there. I won't make it, Burny. I won't."

"You're acting fruity. I said to ignore the jelly in the hallway. Put yourself in gear. Move! We'll wait three days for you. After that, no guarantees. Leave when the moons are down and the suns are not quite up. Pick a time when the shadows are confusing. Are you with me?"

"Yes and no."

"Good. Fill your pockets with gauze pads. You'll need them. The weather is a mess. Whenever you come to a juncture, angle to the right. Follow me?"

"Yes and no."

"That'll do. Remember, boy. Crossing the bottoms is not so easy. You'll be tried. You'll have to be at your most alert. Stay off the stonepicks."

"I'm a little weak for a trip like that."

"Bring cigars. You'll want cigars."

"What about food? Liquids?"

"Food? Did you say food, Moldenke? Liquids? Tell me, didn't you pass the survival exams? Haven't you read the book? Consider the first line: *Starving at home is a simple matter*, and so on. The swamp is a banquet table, son, always set. Kick open a rotted stump. Find it crawling with protein. The right fungus is good bread. It would take a jellyhead to starve in the bottoms. Liquids? Liquids are everywhere in the bottoms. Don't talk to me about liquids. Find a water flower, suck the stem. I fail to see the problem. Take the book along.

Besides, I don't think you have the luxury of a choice at this point, do you?"

"Maybe not. I'm beginning to have fears, Burny, buzzing up and down the spine. What should I do?"

"Nothing. At least you're feeling something. That's enough."

"They'll follow me, Burny. I won't get away so easy."

"So will your shadow. I'm not impressed."

"I don't have any weapons."

"Wrong, Dink. You have yourself. You and Bunce are equally armed."

"I might be safer staying here."

"I doubt that. But go ahead, stay. Wait for the bloodbird to sweep down and pick the bones, show the coyote how soft your belly is. I'll just staple your folder shut and file it away. So long, Dink. *Requiescat* and so on."

"No, Burnheart. Don't hang up."

"Would you be kind enough to leave me your brain, assuming Bunce doesn't get ahold of it? I have an empty jar on the shelf. *A memento mori*, a first degree relic of the late—"

"Stop! Burnheart, don't say those things. The hearts are beating funny. I feel cramps."

"Maybe you'll have a successful dump after all. Why not stop this exchange of jumbo? Are you ready to leave that room? Or shall I tell Eagleman we're dealing with a weak sister?"

"It hurts when you say that."

"Oh, Moldenke. I pity you. Cry me an orangeade tear."

"Don't bother to pity me. I'll get by."

"Thank you for saying that. You think we take no risks in helping you? You think this call isn't being monitored? What do you think Eagleman is putting on the line for you? What are we, a pair of cluck hens? Open your eye. See us as we are. Don't give yourself to Bunce. Give yourself to us, to science, as it were. We have a fireplace, a continuing fire, and a pile of mock wood. Come and sit with us by the fire, eat some of our popcorn. There's an extra laboratory. It's yours when you come. Drink some tea with us. We'll talk about this and that, things. If you get to feeling tight, you can bounce around in the latex room. Everything we have is yours. But our patience is not interminable. Eagleman is not as placid as I am. He's a very busy man, tempered in fire. One day it's the rubber tomato, the next day it's the mystery of autotomy. The man lives always on the rim of a volcano. Be cautious with him. Moldenke? Are you with me?"

"You say I should ignore the jelly in the hall? Is that right?"

"Right. It must be total, though. Out of mind, out of sight. If you think of him even a bit, he'll be on you. You may have to force yourself to think about something else. Get together now."

"What about the weather? I'd like to get a report."

"Once you're in it you'll know. Goodbye. See you in three days or not at all."

29]

During the year previous to the mock War Moldenke was employed at the Tropical Garden as a banana man.

30]

He pulled on his trenchpants and rooted in his closet for Burnheart's old trenchcoat. He stuffed all pockets with .00 gauze pads and cigars, strapped on his sidepack and dropped in flints, a can of k-fuel, a tin of crickets, a handful of prune wafers, and a packet of stonepicks. He buttoned up the trenchcoat. Burnheart had worn the coat in an earlier war and had been wounded in it below the frontal buckle.

In his backpack he loaded old Burnheart letters, blank paper, pens, pencils, and two copies of Burnheart's book, *Ways & Means*.

He gathered his hair and tied it in the back. Still, several moons were up.

He waited in the chair.

The phone rang:

"Hello? Burnheart?"

"No, jock. I think that nothing measures equal to the Moldenke innocence except the Moldenke presumption. No, this is not Burnheart."

"Bunce?"

"Yes, this is Bunce."

"I have nothing to say, Bunce. I'm under different instructions now."

"Moldenke, are you aware of the hazards in the bottoms? You won't make it. Believe me. Consider the odds. Burnheart is far from perfect."

"I'm ignoring you, Bunce. You're wasting time."

"I've been ignored before. I can live with it."

"I'm going to hang up. I have nothing to say."

"Fine, we're even again. I have nothing to hear. But let me say a few things before you set the speaker down. Will you grant me thirty seconds? Moldenke, I can build a wall around you with the details of your life. I know all your secrets. One of your nose hairs is deviant, isn't it? It grows away from the others, doesn't it, toward the brain? There, that explains your snorts. Can you see what I'm getting at, jock? I not only know *that* you snort, but *why*. That's the important fact, *why*. I know you totally. I don't want much from you, Dink. *All* is what I want, the whole Moldenke. Take off that trenchcoat and get back in the chair. Quit fiddling."

"No, Bunce. I'm ignoring you."

"How can you? Test me. Ask me anything about yourself. Try me...pick a hard one."

"All right, Bunce. Several years ago I was in the crowd along a boulevard watching a parade. Someone tapped my shoulder and I turned to see. It was Cock Roberta. The crowd pushed us close. I felt my crank harden against her leg. She put something into my hand. A wave went through the crowd and we were separated. What did she leave in my hand?"

"A little polished acorn opening on copper hinges, warm with her perspiration. *Warm with her perspiration,*

Moldenke! What do you think of *that* detail? Little Cock is a hot handed woman, isn't she?"

"All right, Bunce. When I opened the acorn, what was inside?"

"The crowd was all around you, pushing at your elbows. You waited until you got home, back to your room. You turned on the lamp and opened the acorn over a saucer and a tightly folded paper fell out. You carefully unfolded it and read it."

"I assume you know what it said."

"Ah, the Moldenke assumptions. Yes, I know what it said. It said, 'Capital M, My dear, capital M, Moldenke, comma, paragraph, indent, capital T, They say that I'm beginning to punctuate and that I'll have to seclude myself and rest, period Capital T, They say I shouldn't be looking at the sky when the moons are up, period.' And she signed it, 'capital C, Cock.'

"I don't care what you know, Bunce. I still intend to ignore you."

"Suit yourself. I tried to help you. You once had a wart on the quick of your thumb. You habitually chewed on it and over the years it shrank and went away, leaving a small oval scar. As a boy you stashed coins and licorice in your cuffs. Nothing escapes me, Moldenke. Nothing."

Moldenke hung up.

31]

He sat on the seawall, chewing stonepicks, and watched the first artificial sun break apart and burn out. A slow, dry rain of white ash persisted through summerfall. By winter a second sun was up, blinding to look at and almost warm enough.

32]

The moons were nearly down. He would read a final Burnheart letter and then make for the bottoms.

Dear Moldenke,
    How many wonders has mother science put to sleep?
    As ever,
    Your country friend,
    Burnheart

He remembered writing back:

Dear Doctor,
    I don't know. I wonder. And it keeps me awake.
    Apologetically yours,
    Moldenke

He saw the last flash of moon through the lookout. He went to the door, listened, put his hand on the doorknob. Inflations, deflations. He would have to forget the jelly. He waited, went back to the chair, tried to get his mind to wander off to the acre of weed and pollen. He chewed a stonepick, tied on a gauze pad. He went back to the door, listened. A labored inflation, an extended deflation, and a lull. The feet shuffled back and forth at the door. His major heart thundered, the others ticked rapidly. He imagined himself a bloated fish, dead on a beach. The jelly, still there. He imagined himself a tripodero, racing along the hedgerows. No, still the jelly. He would have to hurt himself. He went to the refrigerator, placed his hand on the door seal and closed the door. The pain was immediate, completely distracting. He wrapped gauze around his swelling hand, left the room. The hallway was empty. He found himself on the street.

33]

She followed the lines in his face with a geographical eye and an imaginary pen, giving each line a name, as though they were discovered rivers.

He arranged a bed of peat bags and they chewed stonepicks. Sounds feathered and nested in silence. She took off the Indian dress and draped it over an elephant plant.

He parted labia with his thumbs.

She said, "What are you doing?" She laughed, peat chips caught in her hair.

He said, "The little man in the big boat."

She said, "What are you talking about?" She counted panes of glass in the greenhouse roof.

He said, "Never mind. Boat isn't right. Canoe. The little man in the big canoe. Cock?"

"What? What are you talking about? I'm not something to be opened like a grape, a warm vegetable. What are you doing?"

"Cock, the little fellow says he wants a cigar. He's all excited. Shall I give him a blue cigar?"

"Give him anything, Moldenke. Please stop talking. I don't follow."

"Yes, I'm sorry. I forgot the T.S.R."

"The T.S. what?"

"The Twenty Second Rule. I've talked about the same thing for more than twenty seconds. I shouldn't do that. My apologies."

"Moldenke, where are you?"

"Here, by the River Odorous. Can't you see me? Have you gone light-blind? Wear my goggles."

"Where am I, then? Where is your temporary Cock?"

"Quiet, Cock. Let him smoke in peace. Don't surround him with question marks."

"Moldenke, please."

"I don't know what to say, Roberta. I have no feeling.

He smoked a cigar. They watched the suns go down. She said, "You've left me leaking, Moldenke. It's running down my leg."

He said, "I'm dead, Roberta. I have no feelings. I *do* like you though, I think. But I can't feel you. My hand passes through the flesh. I see only an outline."

He bumped the ash from his cigar. A moon fluttered up and settled in its spot.

34]

At one time Moldenke enjoyed the oncome of winter, greeted it with a flourish of ritual activity. He was comfortable in a state of cold. Twigs snapping underfoot with icy reports. The air was never still enough for Moldenke's comfort until it was heavy with frost or wet with sleet. When the new snow came he would go out and piss his name in it. As years succeeded, the rituals went on. He noted the fall of the last leaves, the changing angle of sunslight, the shift of winds. He felt relief when the final evidence of green was gone, when the fur of animals thickened. He would light his k-heater, take down blankets, snap in the storm windows.

Once Burnheart had said to him, " Moldenke, puff out those cheeks, please." Moldenke had done that and Burnheart had said, "As I thought. Dink, you grow more like a gopher every season. I know it's not the cold you like so well. No, it's the defensive pleasures of remaining warm *within* the cold. It's that. I know the story, son. Quick to cocoon but slow to change. It's an old tale."

Summerfall came differently. He would watch the earth dry and crack in repeated patterns. Greenbirds came, land turtles walked over country roads, surly grasshoppers baked in the sunslight. Rising temperatures set Moldenke on the offensive, causing him to speed from A to B, from thought to thought, from one thing to the next thing. "Pace yourself," Burnheart had told him one summerfall. "Pace yourself or you'll never make it in the army."

35]

He stood against a building. Occasionally a k-vehicle would pass in the street. The night sirens rang. A woman walked by, wrapped in a dog fur. Moldenke stepped out of the shadow.

"Miss, excuse me...miss?"

She turned and looked at him from the dog fur.

"I'm a stranger in town, miss. Could you point me to the south?" He searched for eyes in the coat.

She turned her head in a certain direction and indicated it. She said, "South, that way." She walked off in the coat, the dog fur, northward, tokens clattering in her pockets.

He backed into the shadows again, considering things. The first light of a sun ballooned over rooftops. He would go south toward the bottoms. He would cross the bottoms and then sit with Burnheart and Eagleman by the fire, eat popcorn.

A double-dawn. One sun from the west, another northeast. The shadows would be confusing. As Burnheart had suggested, he would move now.

He followed alleyways, climbed fences. Things were thrown at him from windows. The running increased his heartbeats. One heart seemed to beat inside his injured hand. He walked, stopped, leaned against a wall, took shallow breaths. A lookout opened. A jellyhead boy squirted jelly from an ear valve, relieving pressure. The lookout closed. Moldenke walked. Another jellyhead lay deflated on a mock mattress. He crossed a wooden bridge, entered the outskirts of the city, keeping the northeast rising sun to his rear left, heading south. Fewer and fewer buildings, the streets tapering into mud ruts and finally ending. Out of the sirens' sound, city noise behind.

He walked a klick or so into the bottoms and stopped. He would have breakfast. Prune wafers and a cricket or two. He would pull together a mound of leaves and tree bark and cypress knots, build himself a fire, warm his feet.

Had Burnheart said to travel by night and sleep by day, or the other way around, or not at all? His hand hurt badly. He couldn't remember what Burnheart had said about traveling.

He ate a prune wafer. It gummed in his teeth.

The fire smoldered flamelessly.

He would travel whenever he could, whatever Burnheart had said, if anything. Whenever the opportunity for movement presented itself, Moldenke would move.

No artificial barriers at this juncture. Always to the right, always to follow the natural impulse. The hum and the flow. Everything was tight.

He lay back against a cypress knee, watched the second rising sun overtake the first. In the city k-buses would be taking jellyheads to work, shifts would be changing, the street music would be deafening.

He ate a cricket, spitting the legs into the smoking leaves, took off his coat. The double suns said ten o'clock, although Moldenke read them as eight. He put on his goggles and the refraction corrected his error. It was later than he thought and getting hot. He took off his coat, stirred the fire. A rooster comb of flame burned a moment and died.

Perspiration broke around the goggles and soaked the gauze pad. He tied on a dry one, ate another cricket, dropped his trenchpants, squeezed several turds onto the fire, pissed away the last of the smoke.

He walked south, chewing a stonepick, wondering if he would clash with Eagleman. With the tip of his tongue he rolled the stonepick across his bottom lip.

He reached into a low swirl of ether branches and took down a snipe. He pinched its neck and dropped it into his sidepack. He would have it for supper. It had been weak, hadn't attempted to fly away. "Nothing here but food," he said. "Burnheart was right."

Had Burnheart mentioned liquids? He would wait. Somehow there would be water, a trickle from the rocks, if there were rocks.

He would smoke a cigar as he walked. He focused sunlight through a lens of his goggles, held the hot beam at the tip of his cigar until a spark caught and circled. He puffed, put the goggles on again.

36]

Eagleman's moon, the first moon, had been a shadow game, a projection of zero on a screen of gas. A mock month before it went up Moldenke learned of it in a letter from Burnheart:

Dear Moonless,

You will soon have a reason to take a look at the night sky again. Eagleman has a moon on the drafting table. The concept of it is difficult even for me to grasp, the way he explains it. Actually, what it amounts to is not much more than a photograph, a slide picture of the old original moon projected against the gassier layers. And he's provided for changing your slides for the various phases and so on. A very efficient, quite portable moon, Moldenke. The man is a repository of mechanical wisdom, a swarm of intelligent thoughts in his head. Some day we'll all look to Eagleman to get us through. Mind what I say. And keep your eye on the sky.

Hopefully yours,
Burnheart

37]

He found himself standing at the foot, one of four such feet, at the base of the legs of a weather tower. The wind picked up, the weather was changing. He shaded his eye and looked up to the top of the tower. There was a windsock, windfilled, a weathercock spinning, and a brace of antennae. He turned up his collar, snorted, blinked his eye. One sun went down behind the tower.

A bank of brown clouds erased the other sun and forced an early night. *Too bad*, Moldenke thought, *and it isn't quite noons yet*. The jellyheads had learned to sleep at will, could doze whenever an unexpected night came on. Moldenke couldn't.

He strapped himself in the lift chair and pressed the buzzer. A voice came down the slot: "Good morning and good night, Moldenke. I saw you coming. Fill up your lung and I'll bring you up. Try to hold the stomach in so we won't spill any food. Have you tied the footstraps?"

Moldenke said, "You know me?" The voice in the talk tube had sounded familiar, but Moldenke couldn't place it with a body, or a face, or a name.

"I knew your name and I knew you were in the area. How many walkers do you ever see in these parts? Who ever crosses the bottoms these days? How many people do I see wearing a trenchcoat, trenchpants, carrying a sidepack and a backpack and wearing purple-view goggles? Who else could it be but you, Moldenke? I said I knew you were coming. I didn't say I knew you socially. My name is Shelp. How do you do? I'm the weatherman."

Moldenke remembered the radio voice, the weather reports.

"You're Shelp? The weatherman?"
"Didn't I say that? I remember saying that."
"Yes. Glad to know you. Call me Moldenke."
"Shall I send the lift chair up, Moldenke?"
"Shelp?"
"Yes?"
"You said to fill my lung. You used the singular. You know me fairly well, don't you?"

"Not at all, Moldenke. I only know a few of your anomalies. I'll bring you up now. Have you got the crotch buckle tightened?"

"Yes, I'm ready."

"Breathe in."

Circuits opened and closed in a box on the arm of the lift chair and he went up. At the deck he unstrapped himself, cricket and prune knotting in his stomach. The ride up had loosened his shoes. He knelt and rebuttoned them.

Shelp took his elbow and showed him into the weather room. A wood fire burned in a floor pit. Moldenke sat in a chair. Shelp threw genuine oak on the fire.

Shelp pointed at the floor pit: "This is where I cook my cat weenies, and sometimes I'll put a naked toe in the coals to clean out my head. You know the old expression?"

"Yes," Moldenke said. "Out of mind, out of sight... Oh, pain, the soap of thought...and so on. I've heard them."

Shelp said, "How do you feel, Moldenke?"

Moldenke said, "Odd and a little rattled, but comfortable, exactly the way I should feel. Shouldn't I?"

Shelp said, "You should. Why shouldn't you?"

Moldenke said, "I shouldn't. I don't know you."

"You may be dizzy, Moldenke. I may have brought you up too fast. Hold out your tongue."

Moldenke held out his tongue. Shelp placed a green spansule on it. "There, that will bring you down." He poured a cup of cherry water. Moldenke washed down the spansule.

The fire whistled.

Shelp said, "Concentrate on the fire, Moldenke. Regard the flame as a reflection of itself. Think of it as hot and cold as well. Play the game. You must have noticed that certain flames do not reflect in certain mirrors. Have you? Moldenke? Are you down yet?"

The teaboil whistled.

"Are you down, Dink?"

"I think so."

"I'll prod the teaboil. We'll have some tea."

Shelp opened a cabinet. "Your choice, Dink: moth-wing, ginger root, banana flower—what?"

"Banana flower." Moldenke crossed his legs and loosened his backpack. "I used to be a banana man at the Trop Garden."

"I know," Shelp said.

"Of course," Moldenke said. "Mind if I smoke?" He lit a cigar.

Shelp said, "No," that he didn't mind. "I'll have one myself." He lit a brown cigar.

Moldenke said he hadn't seen a brown cigar since before the mock War. Shelp agreed they were rare.

They drank tea and smoked.

Shelp said, "I work for Bunce." Moldenke threw his tea in the fire and stood up.

"You work for Bunce?"

"Be easy, Moldenke. Sit down. You're safe here."

"You said you worked for Bunce."

"I didn't mean to excite you. I know it's hard on the hearts. In fact, the tower belongs to Bunce. In that sense I work for him. Frankly, I've never seen the man. I just live here and do my job. He calls me sometimes and we talk about the weather."

On one wall weather gauges gave readings. They watched the needles move.

"They aren't accurate," Shelp said. "Bunce prefers it that way."

A strong wind blew against the tower. The wind gauge read calm.

Shelp said, "You'll have to pardon me now. I have to do the weather." He sat at a table under the weather gauges, spoke into a microphone:

Roving chuff clouds, floxiness hovering above L.A. unpredictable, nothing verified, minimum forecast, probable extensive sunsout, birdfall index high per hundredcount, earlier reports not reliable, premature, lofty hopes for a sunsy weekout, otherwise rain and sleet.

Moldenke slept intermittently. Shelp stood over the teaboil. The wind whistled. The fire in the floor pit died.

"Do you recognize time, Moldenke?"

Moldenke sat up, eye wide. "Where is it?" He blinked away a forming daydream, although outside the night was early.

"Consider the future, Moldenke. Do you imagine we'll ever get there? Some folks see it as a k-bus trip.

56

You get there, you get off, set down the packages, and talk about the chuckholes. I wonder about the quality of that. Moldenke?"

38]

When the government moons went up, Eagleman's moon came down.

39]

Moldenke had postponed the matter of booster hearts until one of his lungs had collapsed.

Burnheart had written a letter:

My Dear Declining Dink,
    It's not an altogether cheering prospect, you moonchild. I sat back and let you be overtaken by a flotilla of polyps. The physician's ethical silence, in deference to your feelings. I couldn't sleep. Never again, son. Where it pertains to you, nature drives in rearward gear. I've watched the teeth rot out, the eye close, and now the heart is down to a slug's crawl. In this case I will not sit back and let the long Moldenke line run out of ink.
    May I suggest a set of booster hearts?
    The surgery is child's work. You swallow the pill and dream about a necklace of planets, or whatever. I'll install the hearts myself. I admit, I wouldn't mind

putting on the rubbers again. It's been a number of seasons. And when it's all over, when you've got four little pumpers helping the big one along, we'll each take home two sheep for the barbecue. Look at it that way.

Your Doctor,
Burnheart

40]

"Another cup of tea, Moldenke?"

Moldenke slept.

Shelp spooned banana flowers into the teaboil. The wind died. The wind gauge needle lurched to ninety klicks per.

Moldenke sat up empty.

"More tea, Moldenke?"

"Thank you. I'm down now."

"Not below the normal level I hope?"

"No, not much below. Yes, I'd like tea. What time is it, Shelp?"

"You do recognize it, then?"

"Yes, I remember the question. You asked it earlier."

"And now you've come full circle and answered it for me. You're indirect, Moldenke. You sniff about too cautiously, like the cat and the recent turd. You parry at the body of something like a timid boxer. Let me see your nose instead of your ass. I don't know what time it is. If I had a clockpiece here it wouldn't keep the standard time, so what's the good of one? Are you in a hurry?"

"They expect me in three days."

"You mean they expect you to arrive on the third day?"

"I can't say. I'm not the one to judge."

"You talk like a cottonhead, Dink. Drink your tea. I'll skewer a few cat cranks. We'll eat. No sense in hurrying off. If they're expecting you on the third day, you don't want to get there before that and find the doors locked, do you?"

Moldenke agreed that he didn't.

41]

Dear Moldenke,

If you place a cup over the ear you can hear the boosters working. As your physician, in the narrow sense, I advise you to do it frequently. Monitor yourself. And, as your friend in the fullest sense, I would say avoid any avoidable excitement.

Your friend,
Doctor Burnheart

42]

Dear Doctor,

I woke up to the sirens this morning with a chestful of nettles. I couldn't avoid it. I behaved accordingly.

It was good to get your letter.

Your patient,
Moldenke

43]

Dear Moldenke,
    Medically speaking, you shouldn't do more
than a sheep would do. The sirens can't be helped.
Imagine yourself in a mock meadow, grazing. In a
stable being shorn. Work on it.
    Quickly,
    Doctor Burnheart

44]

Dear Doctor Burnheart,
    No more than a sheep would do? Should I
assume that the operation failed? I was able to do
more than a sheep before, with one heart. Am I to
assume that the operation did nothing?
    Anxiously yours,
    Moldenke

45]

Dearest Dinky,
    What we're after in this particular surgical
procedure is longevity. You will probably live longer,
though not as well. We're looking for quantity here.
And it also has its dangers, most notably the fact
that if one goes they all go. Or, be satisfied with the
brighter side—since the main one can't possibly fail
until the other four in succession do, you'll have a

warning, an unmeasured period of grace. We should all be so lucky.

Yours,
The one of hearts,
Doc Burny

46]

They drank tea, smoked brown cigars, talked about the weather.

Abruptly, as Shelp was mentioning the possibility of a flood, Moldenke tightened his backpack strap and went to the door, his trenchpants bunched at the knees, adjusting his goggles and gauze pad. "I'm leaving now, Shelp. Would you point me to the south? It's dark. I'm lost without the suns. I have enjoyed the visit. It's nice to meet someone these days who isn't leaking jelly all over. Will you show me the south?"

"What are you hurrying to, Moldenke? Where is it that someone could want to get to? Sit down and act easy. I'll do another weather report. Sit. Don't go off."

Moldenke came back, sat down on a dog bench. "It would be helpful to know the weather. I'll stay for the weather report. Then you'll point me south?"

"Sure I will. I can tell you right now there won't be any suns up for a few days. Government economics, Dink. What can we do? Bees in the hive. You know the story. You'll be walking in the dark for a while. I wish I could help you. I'll do the report."

The wind fence is near completion along the coastal swamps, wind speed down, temperature de-emphasized until same time tomorrow and Sunday, birdfall seasonal to normal...

Shelp swiveled in his chair and looked at Moldenke.

"Something's wrong, Dink. I'm not doing it right. Words I haven't said are coming out of me."

"The banana flower tea? You might be reacting?"

"No, I don't react. I'll try again."

Snowslides at Modessa, blowing flox in Great Chicago metro area, enclose the animals...no fishing in the water tubs...possible flooding on the River Odorous...

"Moldenke, it isn't right..."

"Well, what now?"

"Watch the instruments."

Moldenke watched the instruments. All needles returned to zero. "They all went off."

"Bunce was listening. He turned them off."

"I know the story, Shelp. I've been the hero of it. The next thing to go will be the electricity, then the gas, then the water. You should get away from this place, Shelp. Come along with me. Burnheart would like you."

Shelp went to the telephone and waited. The telephone rang.

"Bunce?"

"I don't like the weather forecast, Shelp. I'd like a spell of moonlight. I'm entertaining a few of the folks

on my k-yacht. See what you can do. Don't be clown-
ing. And tell my pal Moldenke to stay where he is. I'm
sending a man out."

"My apologies, Bunce."

"Enough chatter. Do the report again, with moonlight this time. Get it on, Shelp."

Shelp hung up and went back to the microphone:

*Seven oval spheres in Scorpio according to the charts, probable
deadly Friday, chance of a two-Tuesday mock week, brackish
drizzles in the midlands, lozenges melting in the drugstores.*

"I'm sunk, Moldenke. It doesn't jell."

"I'll take you to Burnheart's. We shouldn't be pid-
dling if he's sending a man out."

"I don't know where the words came from,
Moldenke."

"Ignore it, ignore Bunce. Come south with me."

The lights went out. The embers of the fire allowed
a dome of glow, covering Moldenke. Shelp lay in the
dark.

"As I said before, Shelp. Let's go south."

"No, Moldenke. I shouldn't. Someone has to stay
behind and do the weather as long as the microphone
is on."

"Shelp, the microphone is on?" He whispered.

"It is if the pilot light is lit." The pilot light was lit.

"Burnheart wasn't wrong. He has flaws." He whispered, "Shelp, is that microphone connected up with
all the radios? Is it live, is it *that* live?"

"I would assume so, why?"

"Shelp!" He was too loud. He whispered again, palming the microphone. "Shelp, I'll say a few words to the folks."

Shelp went to the lookout and listened to the weather. Moldenke approached the microphone.

47]

Moldenke had been shrimping in a water tub when Eagleman's moon came down. It first fell twenty degrees of altitude and stopped, vibrated, dimmed, and returned to its original spot. Someone told Moldenke that it had been a seasonal drop, something of stellar influences, nothing to be excited about. He threw the shrimp net again, drew it in empty. Someone said, "No shrimping in the water tubs."

The moon grew suddenly bright, fell to the horizon, held there like a baseball in the mud, and gradually went out.

Moldenke raised the wick of his k-lamp.

48]

"Folks, please pay attention to this announcement. This is not a weather report." He imagined his voice echoing in stadiums, in dark rooms, interrupting jellyhead workers. "My friend here is Shelp. My name is Moldenke, out of Texaco City. It's time we ended our backward ways. Don't be pinned like a flutterby in a camphor box. Get up, go out and mill in the street. What can they do, occupy the rooms? Everybody turn on the faucets. Open the lookouts and turn on the heaters. Heat the city. Protcher a friend in a tender place. Be good. Be sensitive to the flow, listen to the hum. As I said, this is not a weather report. This is Moldenke of Texaco City. Bloodboy, mock soldier, banana man, shrimper—I've done my share of swallowing chuff."

Shelp turned from the lookout. "You're doing good, Dink. Don't get excited, though."

"Turn the volume up, folks. The weather is improving in spurts. Remember the old sun? The old moon? The old songs we used to sing about them? The government sent Eagleman and his moon to wane in the country, sent up its own moons. Up they went, a new mock moon every paper month, confusing the issue of tides. At least with Eagleman's moon we could get to see a sky movie every month. Now, what now? The g-boys give us gauze and goggles, encouraging indoor play. They send out a herd of jellyheads to do the mock work and the rest of us hole up in our rooms."

"Ease off, Moldenke. You're getting me excited. My hearts...one of them quit on me yesterday."

Moldenke switched off the microphone. The lights flickered and went on. The gauges came to life, gave false readings.

"Shelp, you have hearts?"

"Yes."

"How many?"

"Eleven."

"What kind?"

"Sheep and dog alternating, and one calf." He opened his khaki and Moldenke saw the scar, the chest heaving, rippling, ticking. Moldenke went close and protchered a soft wattle under Shelp's chin. "I like you, Shelp. Let's go south. No more time games. He's sending a man out."

"I can't, Moldenke. When one of them goes—"

"I know. All of them go. I know. But you've got ten more. We can make it to Burnheart in time for a heart fix. Pack a few things. Bring cigars."

"No, I wouldn't make it." He gave Moldenke a key. "Here, take my k-motor. The tire is low but it runs. It might get you there. Trust me, Moldenke. Get on it. I'll see you after the flood maybe, depending on the hearts. The calf heart is a good one. It may suffice alone when the other ones quit. Go, Moldenke. I'll broadcast till the man comes. We'll see what happens." He took Moldenke's elbow and led him to the door. "Goodbye, Dink."

Moldenke tightened his coat straps. "Thank you for the tea, Shelp. He sat in the lift chair and buckled in. He turned to Shelp. "I'll be looking for you after the flood."

Shelp smiled, bent forward, holding his chest, went back into the weather room.

The telephone rang. He stood over it and let it ring. The lights went off. He took off his rubber shoe and dipped his foot in the floor pit. As the embers sizzled into the flesh, the phone stopped ringing, the lights went on, and the gauges gave accurate readings.

49]

One season past, Moldenke thought of farming. He wrote off for a dozen chickens in the mail. In a genuine month he received a package of egg shells and a bag of yellow powder.

He opened the *Ways & Means* to agriculture, found most of the section deleted. He turned to livestock and found a picture of a wooden bull, mechanically cranked, ejaculating plastic sacks of sperm into a bucket. Burnheart stood smiling over the wooden bull, wearing his cowboy hat.

50]

Dear Moldenke,

Whether or not you have feelings for me, or feelings at all, I do have feelings about you. They increased when you compared my nipples to pencil erasers. No one has been so gentle to me.

The clouds are promising rain.

Love,
Cock Roberta

51]

Dear Cock,

Although my feelings have not improved, I like you more. Burnheart is trying to find me a laboratory job in the city. If he does we can

be together on weekouts. I enjoy your apparent
affection for me. When I see you I'll play the
Buxtehude. Do you have a piano?
    Your friend,
    Moldenke

52]

Dear Doctor Burnheart,
    In the morning my first duty at the Trop Garden
is to walk the banana rows and inspect the plants.
If I see mites or spiders or anything unusual, my
second duty is to report it to you. Consider this,
today's report:
    (1) Triple the usual number of mites, no spiders.
Normally I see a few spiders. Today, none.
    (2) Leaves facing the southern sun are dry and
fibrous.
    (3) General trunk damage.
    (4) Jellied fruit, if any.
    (5) Dead snipes covering the ground.
    Cordially yours,
    Awaiting word,
    Moldenke

53]

Dear Moldenke,
    We have cause for concern. It is not good that
one branch of arachnida would be present in greater

numbers, while another branch declines. It's a puzzle,
son. Thank you for sending me the pieces. I'll work on
it. Eagleman should know about it, too. Meanwhile,
continue the rounds. Report any further changes.
    Yours in spades,
    Burny

54]

Dear Burny,
    When this note reaches you, the way the mails
are these days, I will have left the Trop Garden.
There was nothing I could do. I'm afraid the Garden
is dead. The snipes are growing deeper. The stink is
driving me off, and I don't have to mention the flies.
I saw the last banana plant crimp and bend over
dead. Something of me went with it, Doc. I won't be
the same again.
    Regretfully yours,
    Moldenke

55]

When the lift stopped suddenly he vomited tea and cat
weenies. He changed gauze pads, rewound his hand
bandage. He lit his lighter and found the k-motor. He
read the tire gauge, had to ignore the high reading. The
tire was low. He walked the length of the tire, spot-
checking it by lighter light, looking for weak spots in
the rubber. Overall, the tire seemed sound.

He threw his backpack up to the platform and climbed the ladder, lowering himself into the motor room through a shaft. He cranked the motor a dozen times. One cylinder fired. He wound the pull-rope and cranked the motor again, sitting on the choke button and easing down several calibrations on the spark pilot. He found a candle waxed to a flywheel and lit it. The motor room brightened to dim, two moths flew in and patterned on the flame. He nursed the key into the slot again and finger-primed the juice pump nozzle. The gauges lit up and gave low readings. Other cylinders caught and fired, detonating unevenly as the motor warmed, gradually smoothing, growing quiet, until Moldenke could hear the beats of his hearts. He caught a moth in his good fist, dusted off its wing scales, and ate it. He turned on the front and side running lamps, the yellow night-beam, raised the volume of the fog whistle. A tree frog croaked in the dark periphery of the motor room. He set the compass point on generally south. He thought he heard the grind of Bunce's cameras. He stepped to the forward lookout, drew back the worn khaki curtain, checking the area. A one-klick semicircle was lit as though in camera flash by the k-motor running lights. He went back up the ladder, through the shaft, pulled his backpack in, closing the hatch behind him. The motor room, except when the frog croaked, went silent. He put the gear jam in very high and the k-motor moved slowly forward, the great soft tire its dominant feature, over dead, doorless refrigerators and rusted mattress springs. He took the snipe from his sidepack, cleaned it, warmed it on a hot pressure sleeve, and ate it. He grew sleepy and slept warmly an undetermined space of time.

56]

Someone shook his cot and told him there was a letter for him down at the mailpost. He sat up, sleep wrapped, rubbing his eye. "Moldenke! Mail at the mailpost. Get it on!"

He stood up. "It couldn't be important enough for a two klick walk in the mock mud, could it?"

Someone said, "I saw government marks on the upper left."

Moldenke said, "Government marks?" He fixed himself crookedly into a set of trenchpants and opened the tent flaps. "It's still raining," he said. "Government marks you say?"

"Yes, government marks. I saw the eagle and the lightning bolts, the blue envelope; I smelled the human glue. What do you want, proof? Go get the letter, Moldenke."

"It's raining too hard." He bared his arm and extended it through the tent flaps, brought it back dry.

"No excuses, Moldenke. You know it's a dry rain."

"I know," Moldenke said. "I know. And I miss the old thunder claps, the water spinning in the drainpipes. Give me an old fashioned downpour for a change. I don't know if I'm up to a two klick walk, blue envelope or no blue envelope. Actually, I don't think I give a snort. The last time I went out walking I stepped into the rib cage of a friend. No thanks."

"Moldenke the pessimist," someone said.

"I had to scrape his heartmeat off my k-boots."

Someone said, "Why do you insist on keeping your old balloons, Moldenke, filling up the tent like that?"

They all struck positions on their cots and read the *Ways & Means*.

Moldenke put on a wet-coat and walked to the mailpost.

Earlier in the mock War he had volunteered for injury, writing his number down on a square of paper and dropping it in a metal box outside the semi-Colonel's office. At morning meal, the day's injury volunteer list was read. Moldenke would eat his prunes and potato milk and wait. When they read his name he reported to Building D, stood in a line at the door. Every minute or so the line shortened by one. The mock soldier in front of Moldenke turned and said, "I'm proud that I gave for my country." He opened the fly of his trenchpants and showed Moldenke a headless crank. "I'm a vet, boy. What are you giving up?" Moldenke was about to admit a minor fracture when the veteran's turn came up. Moldenke asked him, before he went in the door, what he would be giving up this time. The veteran shaped his hand into a gun and pointed a finger toward himself, cocking his thumb. During Moldenke's minute outside the door, a gun fired and someone shoveled smoking bones onto a pile at the side of the building. A red light blinked above the door jamb, everyone in line saluted. Moldenke snorted. The green light went on and Moldenke stepped into the prep room. A table, a jellyhead mock doctor in a swivel chair. Moldenke crossed his hands behind his back and waited. The jellyhead pushed colored plastic wafers into configurations on the desk top. A circle, a cross inside the circle. Moldenke coughed honestly and the jellyhead looked up, turning a knob on his throat box.

Moldenke said, "Moldenke, sir. Minor fracture."

The jellyhead swiveled a quarter turn and looked at a chart of seasons on the wall.

Moldenke said, "Moldenke, sir. Minor—"

The jellyhead said, "You I heard! Weather is the outside how?"

Moldenke waited for the correction. The jellyhead said, "Correction: I heard you! How is the weather outside?"

Moldenke said, "Not bad. A little blister snow last night. Not bad."

The jellyhead swiveled a half turn and adjusted his word order bubble, swiveled back, his headlight shining in Moldenke's eye. "What are you giving up, General Moldenke?"

Moldenke mentioned the minor fracture. The jellyhead arranged the colored wafers into a square containing other wafers. "How brave you are, Moldenke. I just this last minute shot a two week vet in the spine. A day ago I had occasion to remove the longest inch

73

he had. One day that, the next day his life. What do you think, Moldenke? Your minute is getting older. Is a minor fracture enough? Ask yourself that?"

Moldenke experienced guilt, agreed to give up a list of feelings in addition to the minor fracture. The jellyhead seemed satisfied, told Moldenke to follow a corridor to the No. 2 fracture room and have a seat. He waited in a cold chair in the fracture room, flipping through magazines. Music played. In a while feet shuffled in the corridor and a jellyhead nurse came into the fracture room. Moldenke smiled, said "Hello." The nurse sat on a stool in front of him and told him to cross one leg over the other. She scissored open the trenchpants, exposing the kneecap. Moldenke looked at the ceiling light. The nurse, in one experienced stroke with a chromium ball peen, broke the kneecap.

He lay in the shock room under a clockpiece. When he opened his eye the jellyhead doctor stood over him. "How do you feel, Moldenke?" Moldenke sat up and said he didn't know. The doctor said, "Good. The War is over now. Go home. Stay in your cot for a few days and then go home."

Returning from the mailpost he rested on a refrigerator in the mud, his knee throbbing, and read the letter:

General Moldenke
The False Front
The War

Dear General Moldenke,
    Because of punctuation we have taken Cock
Roberta. You may have custody of her after the War.
We have her on a standard regimen. She often talks
about her hero.
    Truly yours,
    The Staff
    The Grammar Wing
    The Great Chicago Clinic

57]

When he woke up the k-motor had stopped, the temperature had gone up. He went to the lookout, put on
his goggles. A number of suns had risen. His forearms
had blistered.
    Someone opened the hatch and said, "Climb out of
this thing, Moldenke, before you fry yourself."
    A column of white sunlight filled the shaft. He
opened his backpack and took out his sun hat, clamped
on darker goggle lenses. "Hurry on, Moldenke. Climb
out of there."
    He climbed the shaft. Someone took his elbow and
helped him out. "My name is Roquette."
    Moldenke squinted in the goggles, saw Roquette
reversed and inverted, a figure in khaki swamp shorts,

boots, carrying a walking stick and a shade lamp, upside down.

"Reverse the goggles, Moldenke. You've got them on backwards." Moldenke corrected the error, apologized. He was not surprised that Roquette knew his name.

Roquette said, "Bright enough for you, son?"

Moldenke said, "A little."

Roquette wore his hair in a back pouch, his beard pulled tight against his face in a net. "Step closer, son. Let me have a look at you." Moldenke stepped closer. Roquette protchered him on the shoulder. "We heard you coming, son. The folks and myself. They decided I would come out and see if I could help you if you needed it."

Moldenke said, "I need it."

Roquette said, "Follow me."

58]

Dear Moldenke,

First, let me clear up a popular misconception. Second, let me hand you a piece of news. One, Eagleman and his moon remain intact. I've touched them both. And two, exactly half of Texaco City burned out last night—old Blackside, the nigger section.

Quickly back to the k-tubes,
Your friend,
Burnheart

59]

Dear Burnheart,
    All of Blackside? What did they do with the
niggers?
    Wondering again,
    Moldenke

60]

Dear Moldenke,
    I'm afraid the plural is no longer applicable. Only
one of them survived, a rangy old one by the name
of Roosevelt Teaset. The rest of them went up in
smoke. They'll flood the area now and let the crabs
go to work. They didn't even bother with a show of
fire-fighting. They simply let it burn. I don't know
what to say. It wasn't news to me. I knew they were
building a fire fence across the city. After that it
was only a matter of arranging a long spell of dry
weather, parachuting matches to the children and
waiting for the inevitable.
    Take pause, Moldenke.
    Yours,
    Burnheart

61]

He middled himself in the auditorium. A dome, angles,
vertical walls, everything suggesting architecture.

Ushers walked the aisles collecting chits. Bunce was in Texaco City to speak to the folks. Moldenke ate popcorn.

Someone whispered, "Bunce," and everyone stood up. Moldenke remained seated and lit a cigar.

Bunce delivered the standard speech: "I appear before the folks tonight with sorrow under my tongue. You have patiently endured while the moons were down for repairs. Now, as together we approach the terminus, I ask you to turn on your flashlights." Lights in the auditorium went out and flashlights were turned on.

Bunce asked if there were any questions. Moldenke raised his hand.

Bunce said "No questions?" Moldenke stood up and whirled his hand in circles above his head.

Bunce said, "I see no hands." Someone next to Moldenke said, "He can't see you. Turn on your flash-light."

Moldenke didn't have a flashlight. Two jellyheads approached and asked him to step into the aisle. They searched through his coats and shirts and reversed his pockets, made him kneel.

Bunce said, "Look at that example, folks. Shine your lights on that man." The audience turned to watch, focusing their beams on Moldenke.

One of the jellyheads said, "Take down the pants." Moldenke took down the pants. The second jellyhead came forward wearing a rubber glove and said, "Bend over. We need some readings."

He followed Roquette into a circle of cypress trees. Roquette said, "We'll sit here and talk." They sat in a two-man circle. Roquette turned on the shade lamp. They removed their goggles, huddled under a mushroom of lamp shade, and talked.

Moldenke said he was wondering where they were. Roquette said he could only say that they were less than a klick from the river. Moldenke listened and heard the flow.

"You look pale and slightly wasted, Moldenke. I presume you came from the city? The cities? How do you say it these days?"

Moldenke mentioned a crumbling house in Texaco City with eastern lookouts.

Roquette described a time when he had lived in the cities, a time when Eagleman's moon was no more than a scribble on a drawing table. His eyes seemed red in the goggles. Moldenke looked at him through purple lenses. A snipe whistled in a gum above them. A delicate swarm of small bubbles came to Roquette's cracked lips and slid into his beard. Moldenke's hearts drummed in the hum of the swamp.

Roquette stood up, his head disappearing into the sunslight, and said he wondered where they were. Moldenke said there was a river close by.

"My apologies, Dinky. I forget sometimes. The brain is always in a fever. Where did you say you had come from?"

"Texaco City."

"Well, a boy from old T-City. Shake my hand, son."
He held out a hand. Moldenke shook it. It was like an
ear of corn.

One sun dropped, the others drifted apart.

Roquette said, "Looks like a break in the weather."
He squatted again and turned down the shade lamp,
patting a gauze pad at the back of his neck.

A blackworm snaked across the footpath.

Moldenke said he was going south. They ate
crickets from Moldenke's tin and smoked cigars. The
temperature dropped.

"Are you chilly, Mr. Roquette? I could build a
fire."

"No thank you, Moldenke. I'll say something
about the cold. As old as I am I may as well be realis-
tic regarding the probable future, given the past as a
stepping stone and the present as a foothold. I decided
long ago to defeat the heat by gathering the wisdoms
of the cold. Once I froze myself crank-to-ground in ice,
read the book, and went to sleep. When the weather
gets good and cold I usually go out naked in my garden
and hose off."

Moldenke built a small fire. "I don't have that wisdom," he said. "I try to stay warm if I can. I hope you
don't mind the smoke."

"Did you say 'smoke,' Dinky?"

"Yes. I have a little fire here."

Roquette said, "Smoke. He wants to know if I mind
smoke. Watch this, boy." He lit a fresh cigar and turned

to give Moldenke a profile. He exhaled at length, then began an inhale. The ash grew longer as the ember burned back, dropping off in lengths. The inhalation continued until the cigar had become a mound of ash in his lap.

"That's a slick one," Moldenke said. "The whole cigar in a single draw. I'm impressed."

Roquette turned, bloatfaced, indicating that it wasn't over yet. He lay back, raising one leg in the air. "Now, watch." Moldenke watched. Smoke curled out of the khaki shorts, out of the fly, out of openings in the shirts. "See, Moldenke. I suck it all in, then I blow it out the chuff pipe. It brings the house down every time."

The fire smoked. Moldenke fanned the sparks with his sun hat. Roquette fell asleep smoking.

Moldenke buttoned on his trenchcoat, moved closer to the firelight and read at random from the *Ways & Means*:

SNIPEMEAT: *In the absence of other meats, snipemeat will provide an adequate wilderness meal. Entrails will be found to contain valuable minerals. The bones may be sundried, pulverized, and taken for heart pain. ....MUDCAT NOODLING: Spawning catfish will generally be found in hollowed out places in the mud bank and may be landed by two people, one the noodler, the other on watch. ...BOX-ELDER BUG-SOUP: Tasty black and orange soup. Two cups of box-elder bugs, sifted, simmered on a warm...*

Roquette woke up, sat up. The fire had improved. Moldenke added cypress bark. Roquette took off his goggles and rubbed his eyes. "What did you say your name was, son?"

"Moldenke."

"Ah, Moldenke. Where are you headed?"

"South?"

"Ah, south. That's a fine direction, son. Which is it, though, the New South or the true south?" Moldenke said he didn't know, that he was looking for two individuals by the names of Burnheart and Eagleman who lived in a house toward the south, some south or another, with hogs living under the house, among the pilings. He guessed it was near a river, or a brackish marsh, since Burnheart had mentioned crabs. Roquette wanted to know the kind of crab and Moldenke couldn't say. Roquette said he knew a great deal about crabs and oysters, had spent a good many years in the business. "But no sense dwelling in the past," he said, making a circle in the dirt with his walking stick and spitting in its center.

Moldenke agreed, snatched a mole cricket flying by, bit off the head and discarded it, broke off the digging appendages, and ate the body. "Roquette, do you *know* Burnheart and Eagleman?"

Roquette drew an x in the circle. "Yes, I know them, in a sense. I went to school with Burnheart, played a little snooker with Eagleman. Why do you ask?"

"Only wondering," Moldenke said. "No reason." Yellow cricket fluids ringed his lips, scales and legs hung in his scanty beard.

"You're a man of the earth," Roquette said. "I can easily see that. We could get along, you and me. Take your nose out of Burnheart's book. I'll take you south in my boat."

"You know where they are, Roquette? Will you drop me off there?"

"No promises, Moldenke. I'll do what I can. I'm not exactly the lord ruler of the boat. The other folks will have to be consulted on every possibility. We'll see. Don't get excited. It's bad for—"

"I know, the hearts. How did you know about the heart job, Roquette?"

"I heard you ticking, son. I heard the bleating. There isn't anyone in these parts as perceptive as myself, Moldenke. Did I introduce myself? The name is Roquelle, with two l's."

Moldenke shook the corn cob hand again. "Before you said Roquette, with t's."

"My apologies, Dink. Did I? Old brains turn to rocks, son. We'll leave it at Roquette. No sense in carrying on any more than we have to. Shall we head for the boat?"

The suns went down, an egg-shaped moon came up above the treetops. They walked toward the river as the evening froze, Roquette's stick sucking in and out of the mud.

"How many other people on the boat, Roquette?"

"Hard to say, Dink. They seem to come and go. You know the housing premium, even here in the bottoms. You might say it was a houseboat."

"A houseboat?"

"Maybe. You might say that."

"On the river?"

"Yes, I'd say it was a river. Things appear to float on it. As a fact of matter it has a name, The Jelly. Do you remember The Jelly from your earth courses, son? You passed the survival exam, am I right?"

"I passed the survival exam, but that was on paper. You never know. I don't think I know my rivers very well, I'm sorry."

"C-minus, son. C-minus. You should know your rivers. How do you expect to navigate? It used to be known as The Odorous. Does that strike a chord?"

"Sure, The Odorous. I remember The Odorous."

"Things change, Moldenke. You stay in your room and never look out. Things change. You should pace yourself. When I was a boy I ate potato peels from garbage bins. A man starts out with ropes to be climbed. Some of them stretch, but he shouldn't give up. Try another rope. Sooner or later you'll grab a tight one. I played some football, too. Nowadays I sit downstairs by the fireplace and look at the clockpiece on the mantelboard. Sometimes I'll turn on the lamp and read the book. Only the tripodero had all the wisdoms of living, and there he is, extinct. What can we do, Moldenke? Things change."

They stood on the banks of The Jelly, Roquette pissing into the thick, oily flow. Moldenke imagined starlight. Another moon was up. At the far bank he saw the boat lights, heard the fog whistle.

A turd washed over his shoe and receded. The corpse of a horse, some of the dray lumber still attached to the harness, floated by.

Roquette pierced the water with his stick. "Good," he said. "It's thick enough to walk on."

They walked the bank looking for foot boards. Moldenke found two for himself and tied them on with cloth rope from a torn shirt.

They walked across The Jelly.

63]

Mr. Moldenke
The Tropical Garden

Dear Sir,

An attendant, yesterday evening, noticed Miss Roberta approaching death in the sun room. He went to her and did what he was able to under the circumstances, although she never was a cooperative patient. Enclosed is a note we found in her pocket. (The note: My diet has included specifically ice cubes, period. A Doctor told me my skin would thicken and grow brown, comma, and it did, period. However, comma, I always refused to drink their soy soup, period. Love, Roberta.)

As you can see, Mr. Moldenke, she isn't herself as the end draws closer. We think you should have come to get her after the War.

Truly yours,
The Staff, etc.

64]

The Staff
The Grammar Wing, etc.

Dear Sirs,
     The buses weren't running at the time. Please
deal with her the way you will. At the present time
I am unable to handle it. However, I did enjoy the
note.
     Yours,
     Mr. Moldenke
     Bloodboy
     Texaco National Gauzeworks, T-City
     P.S. You should understand—I was injured in the
mock War. I gave up some feelings for my country.
She would be a burden to me now, as I am to myself.

65]

My Dear Cock,
     I've taken the liberty of writing you a poem.
Burnheart tells me I should practice my sense
therapy more often. He suggested poems. I've tried
my best to arouse some feeling:

Asking space   Roberta gave me time.
Having Time   I gave Roberta Space.
     While the moonlights sail above the hoeblade,
     The noonlight's mine until the end comes.

86

I touched her face   Taking grace.
  While the sea belongs to me until the end comes.
Wanting a month   Roberta gave November.
  When the end comes, Roberta won't remember.

Sorry about the lack of feeling, Roberta. I hope
you can see improvement, though.
Love?
Moldenke

66]

Dear Dink,
  A short test: You are standing under a high gum
tree, or a higher jujube. Of course, tree taxonomy
isn't the question here. You stand under the tree, as
before. From the upper limbs a bone falls dry and
hollow at your shoe side. You stoop and examine,
stoop and examine. You ask yourself, "A human
bone?" Not a boneman, you cannot answer. Should
it have been a banana, the story would have been
different, if you follow what I say. You vaguely wish
that Eagleman were at your side, knowing that
Eagleman would know the bone as well as anyone.
What do you do?
  I await your answer,
  Doc

Dear Doctor,
 My answer: You step a few paces back and
review the upper limbs, a thought which should,
ideally, have arisen well before this, boneman or not.
Having done that, the rest unfolds:
 (1) Owing to an unfavorable congruence of
seven broken tide moons on a memorable summerfall
night a number of seasons ago, as I recall, the River
Odorous rose over its banks and filled its floodplain.
 (2) In predicting droughts, the weatherman was
off.
 (3) Living things were buoyed up, clinging in
the treetops, including toxic varieties of local snake.
 (4) On man and beast alike, snakebites took a toll.
 (5) The Odorous waters in time returned to time
winding main channel, bright sunlight and carrion
eventually cleaned the carcasses, and now and then a
bone will work loose and fall to the ground.
 Your pupil,
 Moldenke

68]

Dear Moldenke,
 Cocky attitudes do not become you. It isn't
enough to know the Way. You must also know the
Means. You haven't been reading the book.
 The facts of the matter are these:

(1) No such congruence ever took place.

(2) The weatherman was on that night.

(3) No local snakes are toxic, or, All A's are non-B's, whichever you prefer, where A is your local snake, and B is your toxic qualities.

In short, you were wrong, Moldenke. I know how we all make our mistakes. You don't have to say it. Frankly, I myself wouldn't have expected Eagleman to go to such lengths to prove a simple point. Imagine him climbing to the top of that ether tree the way he did, carrying a heavy sack of bones to boot. Apparently Eagleman has a playful streak.

Give my best to Cock Roberta.

Your friend,

Burnheart

69]

Lift seats brought them up to the lower deck, past a vertical row of gaping exhaust holes, smelling of un-burned k-fuel.

They unstrapped and walked the deck. Roquette said, "It's an old boat, son. But she goes good."

Moldenke said, "Where are the folks?" The deck seemed empty, badly lit. "I get the impression no one is here."

"Not so quick to trust your senses, Moldenke. Let me show you around, meet a few of the folks. I'll take you to your room and you can lay down your baggage."

Moldenke said, "That would be good."

Roquette said, "Maybe not."

The river ran thickly by. Three moons were up like pies in a bakery. On the far bank a dog barked. Rubbery water lapped at the side of the boat. Moldenke asked if the boat had a name. Roquette said the folks hadn't been able to agree on one. Somewhere on the boat a toilet flushed. Moldenke said, "Plumbing?" Roquette agreed.

"Slow down, Moldenke. Why don't we sit here a minute in these deck chairs and have a look at the sky. How well do you know the mock astronomy? Sit down and I'll give you a lesson." They sat.

Moldenke said, "Three moons, two more threatening at the east horizon. Looks like a dreary night."

Roquette said, "Dreary, he says."

Moldenke closed his eye and imagined the old moon, large and orange in the sky. Roquette said, "Don't be cruising in the past, son. Stay with me." Moldenke opened his eye. "How many moons are up, Moldenke?"

"Three, two rising."

"For a total of five," Roquette said.

Moldenke agreed. Roquette said, "Now, look west." Moldenke looked west. "Describe."

Moldenke described: "Double domes of moonlight, sure. Two more threatening in the west. I didn't see it before."

Roquette said, "For a total of seven."

Moldenke said, "Seven."

Roquette said, "Yes, seven moons congruent. We might get a little high water tonight, son."

Moldenke said, "Nasty weather, anyway. I agree."

Roquette said, "You are very fortunate to be on this boat." Moldenke said he knew it, thanked Roquette for finding him. Roquette said, "The only floating boat, the last flowing river. Here we are, son. This is it. Are you with me?" Moldenke said he was, icicles forming at the brim of his sun hat. "I didn't know that things had gotten that bad." Roquette said he was afraid they had. "No use carrying on about it, though. Why don't we go on up to the game table mezzanine and shoot a few cues of snooker?"

Moldenke said, "Roquette, how large is this boat?"

Roquette said, "In what sense?"

Moldenke said, "Lengthwise, from bow to stern."

Roquette said, "It's hard to say. I'd have to guess. It wouldn't be accurate. I won't even try. Don't clutter up the boat with questionmarks. Let's play snooker."

They walked for the game mezzanine. On the elevator Moldenke lost himself in guessing at the size of the boat.

70]

Capital D, Dear, capital L, Love, comma,

Indent, capital T, The, capital T, Trop, capital G, Garden flowers were so almost colored, comma, and the poem so close to feeling, period. Capital Y, You get better, comma, capital I, I get worse, period.

Capital W, With punctuated love, comma,
Capital R, Roberta

71]

Dear Moldenke,

The Trop Garden couldn't last forever, just as
Roosevelt Teaset can't. Can you see this? Can you
reason it? It's a terrible loss, but nothing to get
excited about. Don't rush to give it all up. Think
about it. Believe me, it might be worse. Keep the eye
on the sky. You only thought bananas were gone.
No, wrong. Eagleman has one on the drawing table.
Remember the rubber tomato? To doubt Eagleman is
to build a cistern on the desert. In both cases you'll
soon find yourself wanting.
Yours,
Burnheart
P.S. I forgot: We'll find you another job. Be
loose.

72]

Dr. Burnheart
Dept. of Overscience
T-City U.
T-City

Dear Doc,

About the job? I've been living on the street
vehicles. If I fall asleep the vehicle becomes a giant,
clattering insect on a track. If I stay awake it bores
me. I've looked at the same fake crepe myrtles along

the esplanade too many times. Yes, find me an honest
job. I need the chits.

    Your dependent,
    Moldenke

73]

Moldenke,

    At your next convenience, bring yourself to a
Mr. Featherfighter on the Health Truck. Check a
public schedule for the stops. He'll put you to work.
Bon appetit.

    Your employment agents,
    B & E Ltd.

74]

Roquette chalked up, dipped his fingers in the talcum
box. Moldenke leaned on his cue, a junk band playing
on the ballroom floor, folks dancing, balloons floating
up to the ceiling beams.

    "This is an impressive place, Roquette." Roquette
agreed and took his turn at the red balls. The port
lookouts framed five full moons. Waiters would pass
the table and Moldenke would take stonepicked olives
from their trays and suck out the pimento jelly, chewing the stonepicks. He sipped a cherry bubble. He
saw one waiter go into a corner and cough jelly into a
handkerchief, then tighten his ear valve.

    One of his minor hearts fluttered.

"Your shot, champ."

"No wonder we didn't see anyone on deck," Moldenke said. "They're all at the dance."

"Take the shot, son."

"I'm having a heart flutter. Excuse me."

"Play the lay. Moldenke, the time hog. Play it, son. Play it."

"The balls are moving. How can I shoot?" Moldenke shot the cue at a moving ball, missed. "The balls, Roquette."

Roquette approached the table. "We're moving. The boat is moving. End of game."

Moldenke asked if there was a radio around, "To get a weather report." Roquette said he wasn't certain, but that the boat was underway and the weather made no difference.

Moldenke's sore hand began a steady tremble. He put it in his pocket. Roquette said, "Hard to keep things still with all those hearts beating in there, isn't it?" Moldenke confessed his health, that one heart was fluttering badly and that others were running roughly, the timing off. He remembered singlehearted days, a predictable beat, quiet sleeps. "Things are getting worse," he said to Roquette. "No matter how many views I take of it." Roquette said he would introduce him to one of the folk Doctors. "Maybe he can jam a muffler in there and quiet you down some."

"No mufflers, Roquette. I'm restricted to the limit as it is."

"Nonsense, son. They pay for themselves in silence alone. You'll sleep again."

"They took a lung out to make room for the hearts. Luckily it was already collapsed. They would have taken a good one."

"It's an old maxim, champ. A tooth for an eye. You must have heard it. We could all afford to spare a lobe or two of the liver, couldn't we? Take a muffler, Dink. No sense in rattling around like a sack of automatic frogs, is there?"

75]

Featherfighter swiveled and faced Moldenke. "Toss if I mind you a few works before we question you to put...?"

Moldenke waited for the correction. A drop of jelly bled from Featherfighter's wrist valve. "Mind if I toss you a few questions before we put you to work? Ten apologies, Mr. Bufona."

"Moldenke is the name. Burnheart and Eagleman arranged this. I got on at the last stop."

"This was arranged by whom? And whom?"

"Doctor Burnheart and Doctor Eagleman."

"It doesn't make much sense to me, Mr. Bufona. That combo escapes me. Wait, didn't Eagleheart promote a moon once?"

"Once, yes," Moldenke said. "The name is Moldenke."

"Shake hands." Moldenke shook the hand, a rubber glove filled with jelly.

The Health Truck hit a chuckhole; Featherfighter sloshed.

"Someone else arranged this, Mr. Bufona. Burnman and Eagleheart had nothing to do with it."

Moldenke said he was surprised, although he would take the job anyway, whatever it was, if it was available.

"Sit down, Bufona. A few questions, please." Moldenke sat in a cup-chair.

"Let me ask you if you use a calendar?"

Moldenke said he didn't bother. He took out a cigar.

Featherfighter said, "No flames, please." Moldenke put the cigar back and chewed his lip. "You don't use a calendar, you say. I can sympathize there, Mr. Bufona. Six technical months in a single day sometimes. It gets confusing. Do you watch the weather then?"

"I listen to the reports."

"You listen to the reports...try this." He gave Moldenke a dried weevil cake. Moldenke swallowed a bite and said he liked it. Featherfighter said, "You will be a good employee, Bufona. I can already see that. If you can swallow a weevil cake, you can swallow almost anything."

The room widened at the top and became circular, although the floor was square, accommodating Featherfighter's desk and Moldenke's chair, nothing more. He followed the walls up, looking for the transition from square to circle, but missed it.

Featherfighter opened a drawer. "May I read you something from the book, Mr. Bufona?"

"Moldenke. Yes, read it. I know the book myself."

"In 1856 Claude Bernard noted the appearance of cloudy lymph in the duodenum... No, that isn't the page..."

If he leaned over Featherfighter's desk, his face reflected in its top. If he drew back, the reflection remained in the polish.

Featherfighter said, "Here it is: *As a boy I often walked the graveways. Once I kicked open a rotted tomb and bees swarmed out. Until then, in my youthful ignorance, I had thought them dead in the winter. It was an important juncture in my career. I soon began to think in terms of human honey, and it wasn't long before...*" Featherfighter stopped, looked at Moldenke.

Moldenke said, "And so on. I know the passage. Burnheart is exploring his youth for scientific indicators."

"Who is?"

"Doctor Burnheart. The author."

"The author?"

"Yes, what's the point of the passage?"

"The point is *Insecta*, Bufo. The class *Insecta*. Let me read from another section: *Spread the wings of two or three flutterbys over a slice of pinebread, pass under the grille, top with honey if available, a basic recipe that even a...(deleted)... could accomplish.*"

Moldenke said, "Etcetera. I've read the book. I see you have a deleted edition."

Featherfighter ignored him, continued reading: "*As a child I was kept in a crumbling house. I would gather earwigs among the fallen bricks and make a tea. My father taught me to make an ant-trap. My mother taught me the piano. As a student under Professor...(deleted)...I read the book.*"

Moldenke said, "I believe that deletion should read 'Eagleman.' Professor Eagleman. They get worse toward the end."

Featherfighter closed the book, returned it to the drawer. "Would you like to start today, Mr. Bufona?"

"Yes. I need the chits. What will I be doing?"

"You'll be eating various insects and dreaming up recipes. Let's get a frock on you and I'll take you down to the Tasting Lab."

76]

Roquette opened a door. "This is your room, Moldenke. A bed, a chair, a sink, an oval lookout, a nightstand, a radio, a lamp, a closet, and a small fireplace with mock logs." Moldenke said, "Very nice."

Roquette said, "There's a common pisser down the hall. We share."

Moldenke said that would be fine. "I think I'll take a nap and give my hearts a rest." He went to the bed and fluffed a rubber pillow.

Roquette said, "No rest. I'll show you around part of the boat."

A note in greenish ink was pinned to the pillow.

Moldenke,
 I am on the boat. Don't show it if you see me.
 Love,
 Roberta

He folded the note and ate it. Roquette waited in the hall. "Hurry on, Dink. Leave your baggage here and we'll meet a few of the folks. Who knows, we might catch a movie." He removed his packs and left them at the foot of the bed, followed Roquette to the elevator.

77]

Mr. Featherfighter,
    Here is my first report:
    (1) The cedar bagworm does not seem worth the bother of tearing it out of the bag. It is leathery on chewing and it has a tendency toward bitter excretions. However, if one were to allow them to pupate and emerge, they may then be soaked in potato milk and pan fried.
    (2) Halictine bees, dried, make a hearty, bracing tea, good for the imagination. Eaten raw they leave blisters in the mouth.
    (3) The cicada killer, boiled and iced, resembles the quahog of the old days.
    (4) While the robber fly has a disturbing pungency and tends to irritate the chuffs, it does have beautiful eyes.

78]

Mr. Bufona, Tasting Lab
The Health Truck
Your first report is now on my desk, etcetera.
Mr. Featherfighter
Mr. Featherfighter's Office
The Health Truck

79]

There were no lookouts in the Tasting Lab. At lunch
break Moldenke turned to the wall and closed his eye
until the time was up. Had there been lookouts he
would have watched the sidewalks go by.

On the second day of work he arrived early and
found an aquarium on his desk, and a note: *An aquarium, Bufo, since you don't have a lookout. Will send along the
water and the fish later. I'll read your report today*
   Mr. Featheretcetera.

On the third day, when he swiveled around from
his lunch break and found a gallon of fleas marked "for
tasting," he wrote a memo:

Mr. Featherfighter,
                MEMO
   No. No fleas. I have hesitations.
   Yours,
   Moldenke (The name is MOLDENKE.)

100

80]

Mr. Bufo
Tasting Lab
The Health Truck

MEMO

I have read your first report, Mr. B. I find it lacking in seriousness, especially toward the end. I look forward to the second report.
Your employer,
Mr. Etcetera

81]

Mr. Etcetera,
My second report:
(1) Both fleas and *cantharides* lead to self-abuse.
(2) I feel I should resign.
(3) I feel. I feel. Therapy helped me.
(4) I do resign.
No longer yours,
Moldenke

82]

Roquette said, "Let's stop off at the hot room. Take off your clothes, son. We're all ourselves in the hot room."

Moldenke undressed and hung his clothes in a locker. "My hearts, Roquette. I shouldn't be going in there."

"Malarky, Dink. Step in. You'll never regret it."

They bowed under a low passageway, entered a room lit dimly red. Wooden benches, a wood-burning stove, a woman attending the fire, the odor of wood sap.

"Sit down, son. Relax." Moldenke sat on a bench, head between his knees. "Breathe it in, son."

"What's the temperature, Roquette?"

"That would be hard to say. I wouldn't want to guess."

Moldenke sat up. Another heart stopped. "May I have water? Is there water in here? I need liquids."

"Watch the fire-lady. Fire-lady, this is Moldenke. He'll be boating with us." The fire-lady turned, smiled. Moldenke's eye was closed. "Let the poisons work themselves out, Moldenke. Let it come. Fire-lady, get this man a cup of water." She carried a wooden bucket, dipped her hands in, splashed water over Moldenke's body. He opened his eye. Perspiration filled it.

Roquette whispered, "She likes you, son. Wouldn't you say her tit nipples resemble pencil erasers? Moldenke?"

"I don't know." He tried to clear his eye. Her silhouette against the stove light seemed familiar. "Cock?"

"Pardon me, Moldenke," Roquette said. "Do you know this lady?"

Moldenke said he didn't and closed his eye.

Dear Miss Roberta,

Once they said there was nothing to do about the weather, then there was, then too much was done, and now it's out of control. Keep yourself warm, Roberta, no matter what comes down from up. Hide your thinking in the clouds where artificial winds do not exist. I'm sorry, Cock. Excuse me. I've strayed from the middle.

I will tell you about an interesting thing I saw in the papers. LAST NIGGER DIES IN GREAT CHICAGO. Cock, the very last one is gone. Roosevelt Teaset. The article says they'll clean him up, prepare him, and show him in a case at Preservation Hall. I don't doubt they'll also sell popcorn, and put him next to the banana plant. They had stuffed him with twenty odd hearts before the blood rush drowned his brain.

I am wired today, Roberta. I may go on. My feelings are greatly improved. I find it hard to acquaint myself with the new condition, but I don't hesitate to take advantage of it.

Roberta, do you remember the morning I scattered sesame on the window sill and the mock birds came along to feed and woke you up? Remember the night we slept in a rubber house at the edge of a marsh in the worst of summerfall? I showed you foxfire and we watched it follow an army train across a bridge.

Cock, it seems that whenever I'm looking for you, you're out, and whenever you're in, I'm never looking. It reminds me of the ghost crab relationship. He'll crawl to her hole with his claw raised, she'll be gone, and he'll crawl away, his claw trailing in the sand. Then she'll return to the hole, wait for him, grow impatient and leave. Then he'll come back to the empty hole. That's the way they do it, Roberta. And we have doorbells and telephones. I suppose, judging from the younger ghost crabs I've seen, that eventually their periods of being at the same hole do coincide, although I've never seen it happen. Nor has Burnheart.

I don't remember much about the mock War, Roberta. I do have a recollection of being found by a lost dog. Because I could feel the heat of the earth I knew I was in a hole. There were government noises over the ridge, loudspeakers broadcasting airbursts. I looked up from the hole and saw the dog's face, his teeth showing ricelike in the battle light. I pulled him in with me and we shared fleas and heat for the night. In the morning I followed him back to my tent, then lost him in the smoke and confusion. At one point someone opened my tent flap and said, "Go home, Moldenke. Your war is over. The injury qualifies. Please don't mention the particulars. Say you were away at camp and you fell in a chuckhole." Don't ask me about the War, Cock.

I'll close now. I've been writing on my lunch break for a change. I have to get back to my weevil butter and cream of ips.

Some time I'll find your deepest hole.

With feeling,

Moldenke

84]

Dear Moldenke,

I'm sorry to say they warehoused all the pianos. I would love to hear the Buxtehude again.

When I go to my Doctor with shivering, he recommends a coat. The nurses read my thermogram and tell me how cold I am, as if I didn't dream an icestorm every night and watch my fingertips freeze against the lookout pane. I would not like to grow any colder than this, Moldenke. Do something.

Love,
Cock

P.S. They say my punctuation improves, period.

85]

"Roquette?"

"Yes?" Roquette half-slept, perspiration dripping from his toes to the floor.

"My hearts, Roquette."

"Change the subject, son. That one bores me. You act like the only man on earth with heart pains."

"I'd like to leave the hot room."

"No!" Roquette's eyes apparently melted and drained down the cheeks. His whiskers flared and burned to small, glowing stumps. Moldenke blinked the apparent illusion away.

"I should see a Doctor, Roquette. You mentioned before that I might see a Doctor."

"Did I? Who installed those hearts?"

"Burnheart."

"Is he the family Doctor?"

"I can't say. There's no family."

"I see. Then I don't know what we can do. All of our Doctors are family Doctors. They wouldn't be able to help you. I'd go back to the original mechanic if a vehicle went bad, wouldn't I? You should get back to Burnheart, shouldn't you?"

"Yes." Another heart fluttered. "I may not have time to get to Burnheart. They're going at a clip. When will we be in Burnheart's neighborhood?"

"I don't know. I wouldn't guess about that."

"Let me off the boat."

"Let him off the boat, he says."

"Off the boat. I'd like to get off the boat."

"He'd like to get off the boat. You'd freeze yourself. Stay on the boat. You'll meet the folks. We'll take a walk through the arboretum."

The fire whistled.

86]

The taxi man had turned to Moldenke and said, "Excuse me in the back. Don't yell if I stop and pick up that couple there by the stadium. The lady looks like she's in a spot." His teeth had been ricelike, his face doglike. Moldenke sat middled in the back seat, feeling diminished.

The k-taxi pulled out of the flow of traffic and stopped near the couple. Moldenke said he had his doubts about them. The taxi man said, "I like silence in the back." Moldenke fell quiet, doubtful.

The woman knelt over a puddle of jelly in the gutter beneath her, favoring her stomach. The man, professorlike, approached the k-taxi, asking to be taken to a drugstore for a tin of "charcoal tablets" for the woman's stomach.

The taxi man said, "Is it raining?"

The professor said, "The weatherman said it was."

The taxi man said, "Good enough. Get in."

Moldenke sat forward. The taxi man said, "No yelling from the back. I always pick up extras in the rain." Moldenke said it wasn't raining. The taxi man said, "And who are you?" Moldenke said never mind, sliding over in the seat.

The professorlike man pushed his woman into the back seat, sat himself in the front, his breath filling the k-taxi with the suggestion of peanuts. When the k-taxi made a curve in the boulevard the woman, in a stupor, leaned over on Moldenke, vomiting a jellylike substance into his trenchcoat pocket, her eyes like the eyes of boated fish. In the front the professor went to sleep.

The taxi man said, "You in the back. What do you think of these two?"

Moldenke said he wasn't thinking.

The taxi man said, "Watch this." He peeled off one of the professor's eyebrows as he slept, threw it into the rear seat. "Check that, jocko. I don't like the way these two champs smell." The eyebrow fell to the floor, lost itself in chewed pinegum, dirt, and flattened popcorn puffs.

The jelly soaked through Moldenke's coat and stuck one of his shirts to his chest.

The taxi man said, "The k-rules are clear on this point. I'll have to take these champs for a ride through the bottoms. No yelling in the back."

They drove out of the city, down mud roads, down narrow roads of oyster shell, reflecting white, far from any suggestion of architecture. Mock pollen dusted the road hedge.

The professor continued to sleep, his lips hanging on his tie by a strand of latex.

At the end of roads the k-taxi stopped. The taxi man opened the glove box and took out a screw driver.

Moldenke said, "What now?"

The taxi man said, "Now we'll take a walk. You carry the woman."

They walked into a grove of ethers, Moldenke carrying the woman over his shoulder, jelly dripping down the back of his trenchcoat. The taxi man pushed the professor along in front.

Two suns were up, close together.

They stopped walking, Moldenke put the woman down. The taxi man said, "Now you take a walk and never mind what I'm doing."

Moldenke walked aimlessly under the ethers, snipes whistling above him. He sat on a log and waited. He heard the k-taxi drive off. He chewed a stonepick and forgot.

Out of the hot room, dressed, Moldenke's hearts improved.

On a sawdust path in the arboretum he said, "I see you have banana plants. I thought they were gone forever." He snorted, mock pollen on his hair and shoulders.

"So, Dink. Still you have the snorts. You're a plague, son. Just like the old days."

"Old days? You seem to know me, Roquette. How well do you know me?"

"Roquelle, son. With two l's. I don't know you at all. One doesn't need a long-standing personal acquaintance to notice a snort, does he?"

"You mentioned the old days."

"What about them? Tell me, who found whom in the bottoms? I could have left you there pissing your name in the pollen. Consider that."

"How did you know about that?"

"About that? What?"

"About pissing in the snow."

"Did I say snow? I meant pollen. Pissing your name in the pollen. My apologies." He extended the corn cob and Moldenke shook it.

"No, Roquette. You said pollen, but you meant snow. You know about that? How well do you know me?"

They passed a circle of jujube trees, Roquette picking a jujube fruit and eating it. "Eat a jujube, Dink. Put your hearts in shape." Moldenke wasn't hungry.

Moldenke said he was tired of walking. Roquette increased the pace. Moldenke rested on a pile of peat bags.

Roquette said, "Hurry on, champ. Let's go see the wheat fields."

Moldenke said, "The wheat fields?"

88]

Big D Dear Big M, Moldenke, comma,
    Indent, Big Y, You forgot to remember me after the War, period.
    Big L, Love, comma,
    Big H, Hope, comma,
    Big R, Roberta

89]

My Dear Roberta,
    All my sympathy goes out to you during this time of verbal difficulty. Burnheart tells me that these things arise invariably when several moons come full at once. Push and pull, Roberta. Hang on.
    Also unwell,
    Moldenke

90]

Dear Moldenke,

I am not much surprised to hear the details of Roberta's ailment. You yourself are infected with the slugs when the moons are up. Everyone feels it differently. Roberta punctuates. You remain in the chair, let things slide. Myself, a mild reaction—I expel a clot of blood in the evening feces. Eagleman, on the other hand, reacts complexly. He changes. Unless you know him well, you wouldn't at all. One moment rational, the next poetic. On occasion he'll forget his proper name.

Yours,
Burnheart

P.S. Eagleman has something new on the drafting table.

91]

"Yes, the wheat fields. Does that alarm you, that we have wheat fields? Where do you think the bread comes from? Don't be a jock, Moldenke."

"Don't call me a jock."

"Don't call him a jock. Why not, champ?"

"Or a champ either."

"Or a champ, he says."

Three hearts fluttered.

"Off the peat bags, son." Roquette showed his teeth, ricelike. Jujube pulp hung in his beard.

"You're changing, Roquette."

"Everything changes."

"There's a load of moons tonight, Roquette. You're changing on me."

"Eat it, Moldenke! I don't want trouble. I've got a boat to run."

"Then let me off."

"No."

"I'll jump eventually."

"Enough of that. We'll tractor through the wheat fields. I've arranged to have a k-tractor waiting at the vehicle pool. Let's move."

Moldenke lay back, a rubbery vein worming on his neck, his face a paler shade. His lung inflated, deflated. Ceiling lights swarmed. He said, "Burnheart?" and closed his eye.

Roquette said, "Moldenke?"

Moldenke said, "Bunce?"

Roquette said, "What was that?"

Moldenke said, "Eagleman?"

Roquette unscrewed a back tooth, tapped a double-dome from it into Moldenke's mouth. "Here, son. Swallow. We'll get you fixed." He squeezed jujube juice behind the double-dome. Moldenke felt it loosen from his tongue and wash down his throat. "Easy, son. Rest back."

"Cock?" He rolled in the peat bags and buried his face.

"Patience, Moldenke. Give it a good minute. And don't smother yourself that way. Turn over and breathe

112

the gas in here. What's the trouble, champ? Not used to an old fashioned atmosphere? Here, I'll blow you a piece." He took a harmonica from a khaki pocket. "Name a tune."

Moldenke turned over and breathed deeply, opening his eye. The gas was familiar.

Roquette blew aimlessly on the harmonica. "Name a piece, champ. I can't get started."

Moldenke sat up, nostrils flared. "Roquette? What is this gas?" He stood up, his lung taut.

Roquette blew something old and soft. Moldenke's hearts settled.

"You like it, son?" He wiped the harmonica in his arm pit. "I was top harp man in the old days. I'll do another one."

"This is more than half nitrogen, Roquette."

"Two l's, I've told you. You're right. More like eighty per cent. Nothing but the finest on Roquelle's boat. What do you think this is, a nightflying outfit?"

Moldenke lit a cigar. The lighter flame rose high, burned brightly. "Oxygen too?"

"Certainly, son. As I said before..."

Moldenke inhaled cigar smoke, blew it out, watched it rise through the jujube branches. "Roquette?"

"I'll blow an old one. See if you know what it is. I hope it wasn't before your time. Listen." He played a different melody.

Moldenke said, "Air! This is air!"

"Wrong, son. Listen closely. I'll blow it again."

92]

He had been standing in a downtown rain, waiting for
an uptown k-bus. A boy rode by on a k-cycle, skidding
in an oil puddle, falling on the sidewalk at Moldenke's
feet. Moldenke crabbed backward, jelly on his shoe.
A crowd gathered and someone mentioned jellyhead.
It had been his first encounter.

93]

Dear Burny,
    What do you know about the jellyheads?
    Thank you in advance,
    Moldenke

94]

Dear Semiscientist,
    You expect me to dabble in answers to questions
like that? Read the book.
    Busily yours,
    Burnheart

    Moldenke opened the book and found all jellyhead
references deleted, as they had been the first time he
read the book, and all the following times.

95]

"Well, champ. I see you're experiencing a revibration. Welcome back."

"This is air, Roquette."

"And it makes you feel good."

"I have new energies."

"Good. The k-tractor waits."

Moldenke said, "Wait—I feel the pressure going down. I feel it."

"Moldenke, the sensorium."

Moldenke extended his hand. A drop of rain fell on it, drained through the fingers.

They looked up.

Roquette said, "Weather students playing, son. Ignore them."

Gray flox clouds hung from wires attached to the ceiling.

96]

Mr. Featherfighter,

MEMO

You may regard this note as evidence of my intent to resign.

Moldenke,

Taster

97]

Dear Bufona,

MEMO

The road to Etcetera was paved with such
intentions. I do not accept them as anything, much
less resignation.

You may regard this note as proof of my authority.
Chief of Tasting
Health Truck Head
Mr. Feather, and so on

98]

He ate popcorn from a paper bag, looked past his own
reflection in the glass, studied Roosevelt Teaset. He
saw that something was wrong.

Teaset wore an old cotton suit, heavy shoulderpads,
suspenders holding the pants too high, cracked black
shoes on gnarled feet.

He put on the earphones and pressed the button,
heard a false Teaset biography and a snatch of the
genuine voice: "Yowsuh." End of tape. He removed
the earphones.

Cottonfield scenes were painted on the rear wall of
the display, blackbirds flying in flawless skies, casting
frightened earthward glances.

Roberta put her hand in the popcorn bag. "It's a
tasteless display, Moldenke. I'm leaving. I don't like to
look at it."

He agreed they could have given the last one a whole sentence to say. "All he says is 'yowsuh,' Cock. Something isn't right. I'm not sure what. I'll keep looking."

Teaset's hand had been stiffly closed around the handle of a hoe, the head bowed, the knees bent.

Roberta took her hand from the popcorn bag and turned away. "I can't look. I'm sorry. I'll meet you at the elephant yard." She left the Preservation building. Moldenke remained.

At a booth she rented a pigeon, bought a bag of mock nuts.

"Is it wound?" she asked the attendant.

"It is, ma'am," he said, pretending to tip a hat he wasn't wearing. "Set'er down on the sidewalk, ma'am. She'll go fine."

She found a bench, sat down, set the pigeon on the sidewalk. It remained, springs unwound, and it fell over.

Moldenke approached, blinking in the light, fixing on his goggles.

She told him the pigeon wouldn't work.

He cranked it, set it down. Gearwork clicked. Roberta smiled. He told her the simplest things would give her joy. She threw mock nuts down. The wings spread, tail feathers fanned out. Moldenke smiled. The beak pecked the sidewalk, the wings began working. Jellylike droppings squirted from the false cloaca. The wingbeats increased.

She said, "Stop the wings, Moldenke. It's too fast."

He put his foot out to slow them. A wingbone snapped against his ankle. The wingbeats increased.

He tried to step on a wing and pin it to the sidewalk. His heel hit the ground hard, a rising ring of pain traveling up his leg, diffusing at the hip. The wingbeats increased. The pigeon began lifting.

She said, "Stop him. I have a deposit on him. Hold him down!"

It rose several feet, leveling waist-high, flew along the fence of the elephant yard. Moldenke followed it, trying to beat it down with his trenchcoat. He reached the end of the fence and had to stop, his hearts beating fast.

The bird rose on an updraft and whistled off.

Moldenke came back to the bench dragging his trenchcoat through painted grass, kicking a clod of rubber elephant dung out of his way.

She said, "I deposited 50 chits on that thing." Moldenke apologized, held her elbow, told her that whatever was missing from the Teaset display had also eluded him, had also flown away.

They rode a k-bus home, sipped tea of ants, and Moldenke played the Buxtehude.

99]

Roquette drove the k-tractor along the edge of a wheat field. A false sun floated above. Moldenke sat where the farmer's dog would sit, chewing a stonepick.

Heat shimmered over the grain, crickets bounced against the metal of the k-tractor. Roquette put on a sun hat.

Moldenke said, "The wheat. It's standing still."
Roquette blamed it on a lack of wind. Moldenke placed
the fault on a lack of imagination. "When I imagine a
wheat field, the wind blows the grain," he said.
Roquette said, "You are feeling better."
A mock tornado churned at the horizon.

100]

Dear Moldenke,
I am now free to tell you the particulars of
Eagleman's incredible new project, the details of
which now keep him speeding around the clocks,
we've had to build a second drafting table, larger
than the original, just to handle the overflow of
paper. Since his hands are taken up with calipers,
rulers, and the like, I feed him his flycakes myself.
I'm getting to be more of a nurse than a science
jockey, as they say. I only wish I could tap the man's
energy source. This project is larger than the moon
was, Moldenke. Very large. You and I would shrink
beside it. But someone has to do it. Believe me, if
Eagleman isn't up to the challenge, no one is. If it
weren't for Eagleman we'd find oneself whistling old
melodies in the end. Have you looked at the ether
trees lately? Have you studied the burned off crepe
myrtles along the avenues? You sit in your chair
and ignore it, Moldenke. You remain. Evolution
continues, Moldenke remains. You remind me of *pi*,
Moldenke—ever constant. Do something! Sitting

there, gassing the paper weeks away, caring not.
Folks walk along the sidewalks kicking dead snipes
into the gutter and never asking the right questions
at the right time. Eagleman may save us yet. Faith,
Moldenke. Faith. Hope. Have you listened to the
weather reports? Eagleman listens. This project will
probably—

I will have to cut this suddenly short, Moldenke.
Eagleman has fallen over on the drafting table.

Hopefully,
Burnheart

101]

"Yes, I'm feeling better than I have in some time,"
Moldenke said.

Roquelle said, "Good. I'm happy to hear that." He
protchered Moldenke's cheek.

"I've got a good heart idle. I was afraid for the
worst."

"Moldenke, the cloud."

A second sun flashed on. Roquelle added a set of
lenses to his goggles.

Moldenke said, "Weather students?"

Roquelle said, "Yep."

Moldenke caught a cricket, swallowed it.

102]

Dear Mr. Featherfighter,
   This is my last report:
   (1) The scarab is violent on the stomach, causing
depressive angers shortly after ingestion, followed
by a nervous cooling of the scrotal sack and a vague
tightening of the chuff pipe. Not recommended for
general consumption.
   (2) Remove the wings, wing covers, and head
from the leaf-hopper and boil with peppercorns if
available. Press through gauze and spread on pine
crackers. A good cricket dip.
   Goodbye Mr. so on,
   I plan to leave the Health Truck at the next stop,
   Yours,
   Moldenke

103]

Dear Moldenke,
   We have cause to celebrate. Take out the
cherry water. Eagleman is alive. The collapse was
momentary. When I turned him over he whispered
that the bulkhead problem had finally been solved
and he pissed in his khakis. Cheers!
   Happily yours,
   Burnheart

Roquelle said, "Let's park this machine and take in a movie."

They returned the k-tractor to the vehicle pool and checked out a k-cycle.

They cycled on an asphalt roadway, apparently in a tunnel. Other k-cycles smoked by in other directions, k-buses, an occasional k-rambler. A row of lights above led off endlessly into the tunnel.

"Are we under the river, Roquette?"

Roquelle's scarf trailed back in Moldenke's face. Traffic thickened, noise increased. "Roquette?"

"I can't hear you, son. Move closer." Moldenke slid forward on the rear fender, closer to Roquelle's driving seat.

"Roquette?"

"Did you say something, son?"

The tunnel lights went out. Moldenke braced for collisions and waited, although the k-traffic continued in the dark, without running lights.

"Roquette?"

"What is it? Talk up."

"The lights went out. How do you manage it without collisions?"

"Take your chin out of my backbone, son. Did you say a heart went out?"

"The lights."

"The lights? Have the lights gone out?"

"Roquette! These folks are driving in the dark! What about collisions? How do they do it?"

The lights came on.

Roquelle angled into a stopping bay and turned off the motor. "What's the howling all about, son?"

Moldenke's throat constricted. He took off his goggles and his gauze pad.

"Nothing. You didn't have to stop. The lights went out. I was curious how they drove in the dark."

"Stop your wondering. Let it flow, listen to the hum."

"As far as I could tell, there should have been a series of collisions. I only wanted an explanation."

"Poor Moldenke. Always wanting. It makes me a little sick."

Moldenke touched the tunnel wall, found it hot. His breathing shallowed. He took in the gas in swallowed gulps, belching it out.

"You call that breathing, son?" Roquelle inhaled it deeply. "One man's air is another man's poison, as they say. Frankly, I can't stand the gas in the arboretum. It's a funny planet. On the cycle, champ."

Moldenke sat down.

"Up, champ. On the cycle. We'll miss the beginning of the movie."

Moldenke lowered his head between his knees, activity beginning in his chest. "No."

"You said no?"

"Yes. The hearts are acting up again. Could we head back to the arboretum? The wheat field?"

"Get up, Bufona! Up!"

Moldenke remained. "Leave me here, Roquette. I'll find the way out. I'll meet you later, somewhere."

Roquelle took out his whistle and blew it, the sound billowing in Moldenke's ear, his hearts badly out of phase, a wash of urine spreading in the trenchpants. Roquelle looked up and down the tunnel, blowing the whistle. Moldenke fell back against the tunnel wall, eggfaced. Roquelle knelt and felt the heart beats, read the pulse, listened for breathing, stood, blew the whistle down the tunnel.

105]

Dear Roberta,
Now I know what was missing from the Teaset display. I suspected it the way the pants were hanging. I paid a dustboy 10 chits and he let me inspect the old man, after hours. He opened the case and let me in with my lighter. I set the cuffs of the pants on fire. The dustboy panicked and ran off, looking for a jellyhead. The pants burned off, caught the coat, burned that off. The eyebrows flared, the hair. The case filled with peanut gas. Everything burned off and Teaset was dead naked, black, and false. I touched the skin, Roberta. I took the nose in my fingers and tore it off, and a wad of cotton came with it. I opened the mouth and found they hadn't painted in the teeth. I don't suppose they expected anyone to get that close. Now I know it, Cock. What's missing from the Teaset display. Teaset is missing.
Yours until the end,
I remain,
Moldenke

106]

In the old days Moldenke listened to the weatherman, his radio on through the short nights, the face of it green and glowing. The rosy forecasts, the cocksure predictions. If the weatherman said warm, Moldenke opened the lookouts, found icicles in the morning on the faucets. When the weatherman said chilly he would turn up his collar and close the lookouts.

In the old days there was one sun, one moon, starlight enough, and one good heart.

107]

A red and white k-wheel broke from the traffic flow and rolled into the stopping bay, the driver climbing down in white, a sidepouch on his hip. He exchanged three-fingered salutes with Roquelle. "Sir," the driver said. "I heard the whistle."

Roquelle said, "Give this man a hainty-check." They turned Moldenke over.

The driver opened his sidepouch taking out a string and acorn affair, letting it dangle above Moldenke's chest. Roquelle knelt and watched the acorn. The driver said, "He's just about empty, sir."

Roquelle said, "Do whatever you can, Doc. I want him on his feet quickly."

The acorn described a small, weak, circle, then quartered it. "He's perking up a little," the Doctor said. Roquelle agreed. The Doctor took out an envelope of seeds, sprinkling them over the whole Moldenke. Roquelle said, "That should bring him up." The Doctor agreed, opening a milkweed pod and letting the silky insides spill out over Moldenke's forehead and drift away in the wind of traffic. Roquelle said, "That should do the job. Thanks, Doc." They saluted. "Sir," the Doctor said, Roquelle protchering him below the lip. He climbed the k-wheel and drove out into the flow. Roquelle sat down beside Moldenke and blew an old melody on the harp.

Moldenke opened both eyes.

Roquelle said, "Welcome back, champ."

"I have to get out of this tunnel, Roquette. One of my hearts is stopped completely." He pressed his chest, snorted, coughed up a cricket. "Roquette, let me out. Let me out of here. I can't breathe."

"Slow down, son. Stop rushing. We'll see a movie. Get on the cycle."

"Let me off the boat, Roquette!"

"No. We're moving too fast now. Seven moons are up. We're in for some weather. The river is thick and tricky. You're safer here."

"I'll jump."

"He says he'll jump. Tell me, son, do you think you could swim in a tub of syrup? You'll get stuck there and drown."

"What's the distinction? I'm drowning now."

"We'll see a movie."

"Throw me in the road, Roquelle. Help me up, push me in front of a k-bus."

"Nonsense, Bufo. Stick around for the flood. Meanwhile, we'll see a movie, have some popcorn and wheat candy. When was the last time you saw a movie, son?"

"Wait. My other eye is open."

"Can you see from it?"

"No. It hurts."

"In time, Buf, in time. Things will improve. Don't be so afraid of your selves. This is a good boat. We'll ride the flood and sail on."

"Where to, Roquette?"

"I wouldn't want to guess at that. No, I wouldn't want to chance it."

"Push me in the road."

"Don't be silly. No walking in the roadway. No shrimping in the water tubs. You know the game, son. Don't be trying to cheat the folks."

"When do we get to Burnheart's?"

"Soon, son. Soon."

"I don't want to see a movie. I want to go back to my room and sleep."

"No sleeping. No. On the cycle."

Moldenke held to Roquelle's coat with one hand, one foot dragging on the asphalt, a second heart gone, the scarf flapping in his face.

They cycled out of the tunnel, curved up a ramp into a parking yard filled with k-vehicles. Roquelle said, "Looks crowded. Must be a good movie."

At the ticket booth a woman said, "Tickets, please." Roquelle said, "Lean against the wall, Bufona. I can't be holding you up all the time. I have to get my ticket out."

The woman said, "Tickets, please."

Moldenke leaned against the wall.

Roquelle said, "Hold on, son." He searched his khaki pockets and found a ticket, gave it to the woman.

The woman said, "Tickets, please." She adjusted an ear valve, pinching out a drop of jelly into a handkerchief.

Moldenke slid down the wall, a third heart fluttering.

Roquelle said, "Where's your ticket, son? You need a ticket."

The woman said, "Tickies?"

Roquelle said, "Tickets, jock. You need a ticket to see the movie!"

Moldenke slumped to the sidewalk, both eyes wide open, his face flushed.

"Tickets, please."

Roquelle went through Moldenke's pockets, found a tin of crickets, went to the window. "He doesn't have a ticket," he explained to the woman, "He has crickets. Will you take crickets?"

The woman said, "No crickets." She gave Roquelle a pair of scissors, "We do take hair, sir." She gave him a paper bag.

The third heart stopped.

Roquelle snipped off a bag of Moldenke's hair.

They sat toward the back of the theater.

"Moldenke?"

He fell over on Roquette's shoulder. Roquette said, "How can I watch a movie with that going on? Moldenke?"

The curtain opened, music came over speakers. "Moldenke?"

The second heart stirred, the third began a steady beat. He sat up.

Roquette said, "They usually show a weather report first."

The music stopped, a voice came over the speakers.

Moldenke said he was feeling better. The eye had closed again.

The weatherman said, *"Government sun falls on T-City."* The film showed a burned area from a high angle, smoke columns rising up. *"Great Chicago sinks, has to be abandoned."* The film showed an empty hole. Moldenke smiled.

Roquette said, "I don't like that weather. I'll have to give that weatherman a phone call. I don't like what he's getting into."

Moldenke said, "That's Shelp. He's a friend of mine. I know Shelp." He sat up straight in the seat, eating popcorn and crickets.

Shelp said, *"Government relaxes moon control. Moons behave erratically. You are urged to stay indoors."*

Roquette stood up and waved toward the projection room. "Turn him off!"

Moldenke said, "Is Shelp on the boat?"

Roquette didn't want to guess about it.

Shelp said, *"Coast to coast, the wind is dying."*

Moldenke said, "So, they finally killed it."

Roquette said, "Kill the weather show! Get the movie on!"

"They fooled around with it till they killed it."

"Hold the sentiment, Moldenke. Let's not talk about the weather."

The movie began in gray. A k-taxi drove through a wooded area, slowed and stopped at an ether grove. Four figures emerged and walked among the ethers.

Moldenke said, "I've seen it."

Roquette said, "Quiet."

"I've seen the movie, Roquette. I'd rather not sit through it again."

"Calm down, son. Watch the movie. You haven't seen it before."

The camera followed them into the ether grove. One of the figures carried a screwdriver. The camera drew in closer. Moldenke saw himself carrying the screwdriver, the taxi man carrying the woman.

Moldenke said, "They changed it."

The film flickered, the screen went black, the lights west up. Moldenke saw two of the folks sitting in the first row. Otherwise the theater was empty.

"Where's the crowd, Roquette?"

Roquette said he wouldn't chance a guess, clapping his hands, kicking the seat ahead of him. "Make noise, Dink, make a clatter. Wake the projectionist up." Moldenke refused.

One of the folks in the first row turned toward the projection booth. Moldenke saw the face. He stood up.

"Burnheart?"

"Sit down, son. Sit down. The movie's about to start again."

"Excuse me, Roquette. I'm going to slip down the aisle and talk to Burnheart."

The lights went down. Roquette pulled him back into the seat. Three hearts lapsed into half-beats.

The movie began again. A k-rambler drove along slush ruts and stopped at the end of a road. Three figures emerged. Two men and a woman. The woman favored her stomach.

"I've seen this one too," Moldenke said. "My hearts, Roquette. Let me go talk with Burnheart. That's probably Eagleman with him. They can fix me."

Roquette said, "No!"

Moldenke recognized himself. He saw the letter opener in his own hand. He saw himself open a hole in one of the jellyheads. He saw the jelly spill out.

He said, "I didn't do that."

Roquette said, "I beg your pardon."

The movie ended, the lights went up.

Moldenke said, "I don't think I did that."

"Poor, Moldenke. So you don't think you did that? What does it matter anyway, son? They were jellyheads. No one cares about the jellyheads these days. You shouldn't feel guilty."

"I don't." The heart beats improved. He looked toward the front. The folks were gone. "Where did they go, Roquette? Burnheart and Eagleman. Where did they go?"

131

"Never mind, son. Let me take you up to my office. I want you to listen to some tapes."

"No. No tapes, Bunce. No tapes!"

"All right, Moldenke. Easy. You're confused. You don't even know my proper name. All right. You'll get some sleep. I'll take you to your room, you'll get some sleep, then we'll listen to the tapes. I have them in my kitty-box."

108]

Dear Cock,

I've quit the job on the Health Truck. I'll be chitless again, but Burnheart will probably help me out. I've had a few ugly phone calls from a fellow by the name of Bunce. Some nights they keep me awake. I don't quite understand why I bother him the way I do, although I'm willing to believe him when he says I do. I try not to interfere with government business. But it appears that government business is interfering with me. I learned my lesson in the auditorium a long time ago, Roberta, I can't describe what they did to me.

I've tried my best to be scientific about things, as Burnheart would say. I've tried to mock the tripodero, as he said I should. I want to see things as they are, Cock. And I do accomplish that on occasion. Once in a hundred moons I find myself at the bottom of some phenomenon, or I might harness a minor force and use it to benefit. Of course Burnheart says that there are different sorts of science, and that my particular pursuit is only one of many, all of them excellent in their own way, and correct, and just as wrong as mine. He says I shouldn't get excited about minor successes. I respect his advice, I listen to what he says. But, Roberta, the weather is getting worse.

It would be nice if you could be with me, so I would have someone to talk to. I sit here silent, too shy to talk to myself, too tired to leave the room, not that I could if I wasn't. Times are hard. This chair smells of peat. I never see a greenbird these days, and if I do, it shortly dies. The legs are getting numb. If you were here you'd help me with my feelings. I thought I had them back again when I left the Health Truck, but every time the phone rings they fade away. Once Burnheart said, "Dink, one day you'll run out of ink and you'll go out to the ink store and find it closed, boarded up, and a sign that says: CLOSED FOR THE END." This is it, Roberta. My ink is low. This letter may grow weak and end in empty space.

The Bunce I mentioned has turned my electricity off and there's no water in the pipes. The refrigerator door opens without my touching it and there are icicles on the lamp shade. What can I do, Roberta? The chair has become a part of me. When I move, the chair moves. Burnheart isn't writing me any longer. I have to rely on the old letters, a little out of date. Bunce has a jellyhead in the hallway. I can hear him shuffling, inhaling, deflating.

What is my sin, Cock? Have I eaten innocent
tissue, innocent muscle too often? I always killed
them, in the old days, before I ate them. Now
I'm afraid I wouldn't hesitate to eat them alive.
The weather is getting worse. I suppose at some
juncture, I don't know where, I myself will be eaten.
Something will pounce and grind me in its teeth.

I don't know what else to say. I could talk about
the suns and the moons, but why? Look up. See
yourself.

I've imagined myself a private acre. Trees,
pollen. An occasional red-eyed rabbit. A place to go.
A soft wind blowing. A sky with color, no trace of
architecture. Sometimes I succeed in getting there. I
walk there in peace for a while, until something with
claws spits clots from the bush.

I hope to see you soon.

Love,

Moldenke

109]

Roquette opened the door and Moldenke went in.

"Good night, son. Sleep now. I'll see you in the
morning." He closed the door.

Moldenke lay in the bed, his head sunk in the rubber pillow, his hearts idling smoothly. The sway of the
boat kept him awake. He turned on the radio, got a
weather report:

Two suns cooling at the horizon, restless moons, animals should be sheltered, travelers are warned, all craft should return to port, possible flood on The Jelly, toxic snakes in the treetops, the wind alive again, temperatures will...

Static interfered, the signal weakened. He moved the dial. Further static, then dead air.

He went to the lookout. Seven moons up, all full. A strong wind blew against the boat.

He strapped on his backpack, his sidepack, tied on double gauze pads, put on a moon hat.

He stepped into the hallway, walked to the elevator, pushed the button, waited. The elevator didn't come. He took the stairs to the mezzanine. The boat dipped forward, snooker tables slid against one another, balls rolled over the floor. He looked down from the mezzanine. The ballroom was empty. He called out, "Roberta?"

He would look for Burnheart and Eagleman. He ran down hallways knocking on doors, "Burnheart?"

The major heart expanded in its cavity.

In the arboretum he sat on peat bags and breathed air. Banana plants were bent over dead, jujube fruit scattered along the paths. "Roberta? Eagleman?"

He climbed stairs to deck level.

The wind increased.

He buttoned his trenchcoat and jumped.

110]

Dear Roberta,

   I am calm now, though doubtful about the
outcome. I jumped from the boat and rode an old
refrigerator up to the bank. I've built a little fire
here. I was lucky to find a rotted camphor full of
root grubs, bitter as they were. I was hungry enough
to forget their minor flaws. The gases are cold
tonight, Roberta, and my fingers are stiff. I can see
my own reflection in the flames, if I look. Myself.
Moldenke of T-City, air starved, yellow, and burning
cold.

   The Jelly is apparently rising behind me. I
could sit here and wait for it to cover me or move
on, I don't know. Now that I have a few feelings to
consider, and attitudes, decisions are more difficult.
I suppose I'll step wherever I see a dry spot.
Whenever The Jelly nips at my heels, I'll take a
forward step. I'll get along.

   I am uncertain where you are, or if, or whether
this note will ever find you. If you are on the boat,
please enjoy your trip and say hello to the folks. If
you've left the boat, if you were on it, and I hope you
have, we'll probably bump knees in the dark very
shortly.

   As far as my whereabouts are concerned, I have
none. I see dead ethers around here, and weak snipes
hanging in the branches. For all the world, it looks
like the bottoms again. The boat doesn't seem to

have traveled any distance. At best I can say that I am here, although I don't know where. I am at large and about.

What else to say, Cock? Carry on. I'll be seeing you again. At the moment my hearts are beating well, period.

As always,
I remain,
Moldenke